Table of Contents

I0694730

CHAPTER ONE

Pedra, I don't know about this. You know I don't like blind dates." Pedra holds the door open for Cleopatra before responding to her concerns.

"Cleo, stop it. You know I would never set you up with an ugly guy." Cleo secretly rolls her eyes at her co-worker's shallowness. For some reason, Pedra thinks that having good looks is the most important trait when it comes to dating someone. Sure, being handsome is always a plus, but the real prize is not what's on the outside, but what's on the inside instead. *Pedra will never understand that, though.*

"See! Girl, what did I tell you? Ain't Connor's brother cute?" Pedra points at a table near the far side of the small bar. A fake smile creeps across Cleo's face, followed by a brief head nod. Pedra and Cleo's dates stand to their feet once they spot the ladies approaching their drink-covered table. Cleo nervously adjusts her black spaghetti strapped dress. *People claim dark colors make you look thinner.*

"Hey, baby!" Pedra exclaims, grabbing her beau as soon as she's close enough to do so. He sticks his tongue down her throat as if no one else is around. Cleo looks away awkwardly.

"Umm, I'm Donte," the other guy says, sticking his hand out nervously to greet an uncomfortable Cleo. She extends hers to shake.

"Cleopatra." Donte makes a weird face.

"Oh wow— Cleopatra? As in the chick from Egypt?"

"Queen," Cleo corrects him.

"Excuse me?"

"Queen… Cleopatra was a queen, not a chick." Donte chuckles while glancing at Connor.

"Yeah— queen— my bad." He shakes his head with a facetious tone.

Pedra picks up on the slight friction instantaneously. She quickly intervenes, "How about we have a seat so that we can order? I'm starving. I haven't eaten all day." Connor slides Pedra's chair from underneath the table. She thanks him before easing down into it. Cleo watches Donte flop down in his seat without bothering to participate in the chivalrous act. Cleo narrows her eyes at him.

Pedra glances at her worriedly, "Hey, girl. You OK?"

"Peachy," she spits out while turning her back on the occupants of the table. "I'm headed to the bar. I need a drink."

Cleo sashays alone towards the part of the bar with the least number of patrons. She slides her ass in the tiny bar stool.

"What'll it be?" The unfriendly lady behind the bar exclaims with her hand smashed against her hip.

"Long Island, top shelf," Cleo replies without looking at the rude bartender. She learned a long time ago to never engage with people that carry around that much negative energy. *That shit is contagious.*

While waiting for her beverage, Cleo takes a good glance at the different characters inhabiting the bar. Most folks look like regulars, and others look like they were searching for a stiff stress reliever after a long day at the office. Even though this spot is a few blocks away from her job, this is still her first time visiting. That's probably because she just started at her new building a few weeks back. Even if that wasn't the case, however, this isn't the place for her. Actually, no public place is. Cleo loves the comforts of being at home.

"Top shelf Long Island; That'll be 15 bucks." Cleo removes her debit card from her clutch purse and slides it to the lady, "We don't take cards for anything under 20 dollars."

"Well, just open a tab for me then."

"No need, I got this," Donte says from over Cleo's shoulder. He pushes a 20-dollar bill towards the woman, "And keep the change." The bartender scurries away with Donte's money before he changes his mind. Cleo puts her card away.

"Thanks," she mumbles dryly. Donte sits down next to her.

"Don't mention it." They bask in awkward silence. Cleo sips from her drink, "Look, I'm sorry if I came off as an asshole. It's been such a long time since I tried this dating thing."

"Really?" Cleo asks, somewhat faking her interest.

"Yeah. I was overseas for a while. I just got back to the states a few months ago."

"Overseas? You were in the service?"

"No, I played basketball." Cleo makes an impressed face while taking in his body's height.

"He doesn't seem that tall," she thinks, but shrugs it off immediately.

"Wow, that sounds pretty dope."

"It was. I missed home, though. I missed it a lot." She nods her head after he says something relatable. He turns his body towards hers, "Do you know what I missed so much about it?"

"No. What?"

"The women." Cleo shakes her head at his simple answer. He continues, "Black women in particular. They are some of the most beautiful creatures on the planet."

"Mmhmm," Cleo hums, not sure what else to say besides that. She noticeably unplugs from their conversation. Donte sighs.

"See, I'm awful at this. Maybe I should stop while I'm ahead." He stands to his feet, "Have a good night, Cleopatra." He attempts to walk away. Cleo grabs his arm.

"Donte, don't feel bad. If I can be honest with you, I haven't dated in a long time, either. And don't take my lack of interest too personally. Knowing me, I was probably going to find something wrong with you even if you were the perfect guy. That's what I do." Donte makes a relieved face while easing back into his chair. He grins at Cleo.

"Don't be so hard on yourself. You seem pretty cool to me."

"Don't be so sure. The night is still young."

***

"Shut the hell up! You and your brother did not do that!" Cleo laughs at Donte's unbelievable story. He laughs, too.

"Girl, I'm telling you! We were so upset about them booing us at the school talent show that we mooned the whole crowd. We got a lengthy suspension for it, but it was definitely worth it. Till this day, we're still known as the Moonin' Millers. We went down in history that night." Cleo laughs again while slurping up her fourth Long Island. She stares down at the empty glass.

"Whew! I think I'm done after this one. I passed my 'two drink maximum' two drinks ago."

"Why only two drinks?"

"Well, I don't like getting that wasted in public. Plus, drinking and driving is a no-no."

"But you didn't drive, though, right?" Donte questions. Cleo gestures that he is correct.

"Hey, girl. I'm about ready to call it a night. Are you ready to go?" Pedra inquires, walking up with Connor on her arm. Cleo shoots her a buzzed glare.

"I need to be. I had a lot to drink-"

"I'll take her home." Donte jumps at the idea of chauffeuring Cleo. Pedra looks taken aback by his eagerness.

"Cleo, is that alright with you?"

Even though she prefers to leave with the person she came with, Cleo can tell Pedra wants to spend some alone time with her man. Cleo reluctantly comments that it is. Pedra stares at her for a few more seconds before leaning forward to hug her.

"Ok. Call me as soon as you get home, OK?"

"OK."

Pedra grins at Cleo and waves at Donte. Cleo watches her and Connor leave out of the door. Donte sticks his hand out for Cleo, "Shall we?"

CHAPTER TWO

"So, this is your place, huh?" Donte asks as soon as they step foot in her apartment's entrance. She tosses her keys on a wooden desk near the door.

"What gave it away?" She inquires, deciding to be a smart aleck. Donte smacks his lips at her.

"What I'm trying to say is it's nice. I really love your African motif." Cleo kicks off the high heels that are currently making her life a living hell. She glances around at all of her tribal prints, masks, and patterns dominating her space.

"Thanks. I have a thing for our people and our culture. It really moves me." Donte acts interested in what she's saying while taking a giant step towards her. He uninvitedly invades her personal space. Cleo instantly feels weird.

"Ya kinda close, don't you think?" She asks, trying her best not to appear intimidated by his unauthorized act. He looks her up and down slowly.

"Yeah… why? Does that bother you?" Cleo giggles nervously.

"It's not that it bothers me, it's just a little unexpected, that's all."

"Unexpected?" He asks, placing his hand on her waist, "Unexpected like this?" He leans in to kiss her, but she dodges it by taking a startled step back.

"Donte! What are you doing?" Cleo expresses in an offended tone.

"What does it look like? I'm trying to kiss you."

"Why? I never told you that was OK."

"You didn't have to. You gave me enough hints at the bar." Confusion floods Cleo's face.

"At the bar? What the hell are you talking about? I did no such thing!" Donte chuckles.

"Yeah right! You were practically begging me to fuck you." He lightens the tone of his voice to mimic Cleo, "Yeah, I haven't been on a date in forever, either… I'm fucked up. I run away every man I meet… Yes Donte, I'm embarrassed by my weight. I need a good-looking guy like you to make me feel good about myself." Cleo's eyes widen from his blatant disrespect.

"You know what? You are a total asshole! I never said any of that! You need to leave," she spits out angrily. She stomps towards the front door, but Donte stops her before she reaches it.

"Hold up— You invited me in here! Now, you want me to leave without getting what we both know you were going to give me, anyway? Especially after all of those drinks I bought you!"

"GET OUT!" Cleo yells at the top of her lungs. Donte jumps at her tone. He decides to leave before her neighbors hear the commotion and call the cops. She holds the door open for him while he walks out. He turns to face her before completely crossing the threshold.

"Call me after you get out of your feelings. Even though you're bigger than I like 'em, you're still a cute broad. I'll rock your world."

Cleo shoves Donte the rest of the way out of her place before slamming the door. The tears burst from her eyes as soon as the coast is clear. She wipes her face while leaning against the door.

"I'm never dating again."

***

"Oh my God! I'm so, so sorry! I swear, if I would've known Donte was such a jerk, I never would've-"

"It's OK, Pedra. I'm alright. I'm just glad he revealed who he truly was before we made it to the bedroom. I would've felt 10 times worse if I would've fucked him." Pedra stares at Cleo surprisingly.

"Wait a damn minute— you were really planning on screwing Donte?" Cleo shushes her as their co-workers curiously look their way. Cleo grabs Pedra by the arm and leads her to a less crowded space.

"Would you mind keeping it down! The last thing I need is my peers thinking I'm some dick-crazed whore."

"Who? Amy and Brenda? Fuck those bitches, they ain't nobody."

"They may not be nobody to you, but I don't know them! I just got here, remember? So, I would really love it if my personal business stayed personal."

"Sorry, girl. My bad, I got you," Pedra steps closer to her, "But for real, though… You were going to fuck Donte?" She glares at Cleo nosily. Cleo sighs.

"If you really must know… I thought about it." Pedra gets giddy like they're gossiping in the bathroom in grade school. Cleo looks around embarrassingly, "Would you calm down! What's the matter with you?"

"I knew it! I knew it— Brother is fine, right?" Cleo agrees with Pedra, even though she hates doing so. Pedra huffs loudly, "Too bad his gorgeous ass had to be a total douchebag."

"What's the deal with you and Connor? You two seem pretty into each other." Cleo purposely changes the subject. Pedra blushes at the question.

"Connor and I have been dating for about three months now. I don't know, I really like him." She smiles at the thought of him. Cleo smiles, too.

"I can tell. I'm really happy for you, Pedra. After what you went through with Anthony, you deserve someone that's going to love you the right way." Pedra rolls her eyes after Cleo mentions her ex.

"Girl, tell me about it! Those were the worst two years of my life! I actually allowed that fuckboy to break me down so badly that I had to change jobs. No dick should have that type of power."

"Amen. Besides, I missed you after you left. They should've kept you and moved that asshole." Pedra gestures that she agrees.

"I used to think the same thing, but now I'm glad I left. It felt good to start over, you know? Plus, there are more opportunities to advance here than there were at the other building. You see how far I've climbed the company ladder and I've only been here a year and a half. Imagine what you can do in that time." Cleo thinks about Pedra's words while finishing her sparkling water. She tosses its can in the wastebasket.

"I guess it's good I left, too, then. Since I don't plan on having a personal life anytime soon, a six-figure gig is exactly what I need to keep myself preoccupied."

Pedra gives her friend a high five as if she approves of her message, "Okurrr!"

After chatting a little more over lunch, Pedra leads Cleo to her workstation. They both sit down at Pedra's small desk to continue Cleo's training. Pedra hands her a stack of papers, "So, do you think you can plug these figures in the system from start to finish?" Cleo nods her head yes quickly, even though her confidence isn't at its highest. Pedra sits the documents in front of her computer before sliding to the side. Cleo uses her rolling chair to take her spot, "Ok, girl. Let's see what ya got."

***

"I think I'm done," Cleo says after entering the last digit onto the worksheet. Pedra looks up from her social media scrolling.

"Really? Let me check it out."

Cleo eases to the side while Pedra takes over. She shuffles through the papers quickly, comparing the data on the screen to the information in front of her. Cleo tries her best not to appear nervous, even though she's secretly holding her breath. A huge grin appears on Pedra's face.

"Good shit, Cleopatra! You've finally mastered the tedious bullshit known as my job."

Cleo laughs, "Wow! That was easier than I thought!"

"I told you it would be."

Cleo secretly pats herself on the back. She lets out a huge sigh of relief, "So, what happens now? Will they finally give me my own desk?"

Pedra shakes her head no, "Not exactly. Even though you learned the computer part in record time, you still have more training to do, and I don't mean to scare you girl, but what's coming up next is the hardest part of this job." Cleo's conquered feeling is now short-lived.

"Hardest? I thought what you've been teaching me is as tough as things get around here? Now, you're telling me that I have to learn more formulas, equations, and shit? How am I going to remember all of that?" Pedra giggles at Cleo's outburst.

"No, I didn't say the work was hard, I said the training was hard." Cleo looks perplexed. Pedra closes the gap between them to talk privately, "The next part of your training is about the contents of this building. The different departments, who you should call when you need a certain document, who you send certain information to— shit like that." Pedra's explanation does nothing to help Cleo's confusion.

"I don't get it. What's so hard about getting to know the building?"

"It's not the sightseeing part that's tricky, it's who you're going sightseeing with. My boss will be taking you around, and I'm telling you, he's no walk in the park. Trainees have quit in the past because of him. He knows his shit, but he's unpleasant as fuck. I'm telling you, I almost didn't survive myself. He's that intimidating. All that I can say is, be careful, girl."

CHAPTER THREE

"Umm, Mr. Bradshaw?" His secretary hesitates to say after she inches his office door open. Cleo watches the young lady stick her head inside before fully committing to going in. She walks towards him after being signaled to do so. Cleo follows her.

"Sir, this is Cleopatra Strong. She's the newest analyst sent over from-"

"I know where she's from. Leave us," he spits out without bothering to look up from his computer. His secretary hurries off without saying another word. Cleo's eyes follow the startled lady until she disappears from her sight. She looks in Mr. Bradshaw's direction, slightly surprised to find him gawking at her. He takes her entire body in from head to toe before acknowledging her.

"I'm not into wasting time, so I'll cut to the chase: I'm going to show you around, but that doesn't mean I'm your tour guide. I hold the head chair underneath the assistant director, so that makes me your boss— if this job isn't too much for you, that is." He cockily stands to his feet. He moves his 6 '2 frame to the front of his desk and leans on it, "Do you think you will be able to cut it, Mrs. Strong?" He stares her down, prompting her to do the same thing to him. His brown, chiseled jaw tightens from the room's tension. Cleo folds her arms with a smirk.

"My name is Ms. Strong, not Mrs… and of course I can cut it. That's nowhere near a concern of mine, so you shouldn't concern yourself with that, either." He smirks, too.

"Oh, is that right? I'm glad you have confidence in yourself *Ms.* Strong, but I'll be the judge of that." She narrows her eyes at his back while he walks to the other side of his desk. He eases into his brown leather chair, looking up at her once he gets comfortable. "So, do you have any questions for me?"

"Just one," she says, taking a step in his direction, "When do we start?"

***

"Girl, you did not give him that much attitude!" Cleo holds her phone to her ear with one hand and her remote control in the other. She flips through her TV's channels, but nothing is grabbing her attention.

"Pedra, come on now, you know me! You know I couldn't let him talk to me like that."

"I hear you girl, but I've seen him fire people for less. I told you to be careful-"

"And I will! I'm a damn good employee and an asset to any company, but I'll be damned if I allow some pompous douchebag the satisfaction of making me feel small so that he can feel better about his measly existence." Pedra sighs after Cleo's outburst but doesn't comment on it. Cleo feels bad.

"Look, I'm grateful for everything you've done— really girl, I am. I appreciate your referral and your written recommendation after getting them to pull my transfer application. I also appreciate you taking the time out of your busy schedule to make sure I got this work shit down pat. I guess I can do a better job of making sure I don't ruin your good name after you've stuck your neck out so far for me. That's the least I can do."

"Thanks, Cleo. I didn't want to say that, but that's exactly how I was feeling." Cleo grins.

"I got you, girl. Don't worry about it. I promise to behave." Pedra feels relieved.

"So! Now that we got past all of the technical stuff, let's talk about the juicy shit." Cleo rolls her eyes at the phone. *She already knows where this conversation is going.* "When I first told you about my boss, what did you think he would look like?" An image of Mr. Bradshaw flashes across her mind.

"Not that!" Cleo exclaims. Pedra giggles.

"I know, right! When I first got there and heard about how terrible he was, I just knew he was some old ass white man. I didn't expect there to be a handsome young brother on the other side of that office door when I opened it."

"Handsome? I wouldn't say all of that," Cleo fibs. Pedra picks up on her deceit immediately.

"Bitch, please! He may have the personality of a warped piece of wood, but Mr. Bradshaw is fine. I can't even lie." Cleo sighs loudly.

"Well, I guess I can sorta see why you would say that. He is tall and he does wear his clothes well…"

"And he's gorgeous! Don't forget that part!" Both women laugh.

"Oh please, Pedra. You think every guy is fine." She gasps offensively.

"I beg your pardon! Just because I find desirable traits in most men's appearances doesn't mean I think they're all fine!"

"Mmhmm… whatever you say." Both women laugh again.

Pedra's phone beeps, "Oh girl, I gotta go. Connor is calling me." Cleo can hear the smile that accompanies Pedra's words. A slight feeling of envy fills her chest.

"Gone head. I have some things I have to do, anyway. I'll talk to you later."

Cleo takes a deep breath after hanging up the phone. She has no idea why she feels the need to mislead her friend every time they get off of their call. Cleo doesn't have anything to do, she never does. Her nights usually consist of her watching the television with a glass of wine glued to her hand until she falls asleep on the couch. Then, at around midnight, she'll make her way to her cold, king-sized bed. She does it so much that it's become a ritual... *An extremely depressing ritual.*

Tonight will be no different and Cleo sighs at the realization. *"Cleopatra, you're pathetic."*

CHAPTER FOUR

"You're late."

Cleopatra glances at her phone, "What do you mean? It's 8:00 on the dot."

"Exactly. You're supposed to be in the office at least 15 minutes early to prepare for your day. By 8:00, your fingers should be typing or making calls. We don't pay people to lollygag."

Cleo stares at Mr. Bradshaw with a challenging glare, but keeps her mouth locked shut. She promised Pedra she would behave, so that's exactly what she's going to do. That's not going to stop her from cussing his ass out in her head, though.

...And believe me, she has several colorful euphemisms for this asshole.

"I apologize, Mr. Bradshaw. I was unaware of that practice, but now that I am aware, I'll govern myself accordingly."

"Good," he spits out before turning his back on her to grab something from his desk. She raises both her hands to the back of his neck as if she could choke him. She drops them quickly once he faces her again.

"Let's go. You've made us both late. I'm supposed to be in the processing department by now making sure no one is stealing from the company. They're on the clock, so they should be working."

He tugs at his office door to open it. He doesn't hold it ajar for Cleo, allowing the door to close in her face in an impolite way. She angrily grinds her teeth when the strong urge to tell his rude ass off engulfs her. Instead, she reminds herself about her promise to Pedra over and over again until she calms down. She swings the door open after collecting herself. She spots Mr. Bradshaw at the end of the hallway staring impatiently in her direction. She walks towards him.

"Is there a problem?" He asks facetiously. Cleo forces a smile.

"No, not at all, Mr. Bradshaw." He nods as if he approves of her answer.

"I didn't think so. Follow me."

***

"Only call them if you can't reach me. If you need anything from processing, I should be the first to know about it." Cleo nods her head at the information. She stares at the nervous processing department supervisor fiddling with her fingers. Cleo is taken aback by how frightened she seems of Mr. Bradshaw. He glances at the employees sitting at their desks behind the supervisor, prompting him to take a dominating step towards her.

"I count at least three people not logged onto their computers yet," he glances at his watch, "And it's 8:15. Why is that?"

The woman takes an anxious look behind her. She hesitates to find an answer, "Did I make the wrong decision by promoting you, Ursula?"

"Um, no- no sir, Mr. Bradshaw." He steps closer to her like he's trying to intimidate her with his presence.

"Well, why haven't they been written up yet? Company policy states that all workers should be performing productive duties at their start times. You do know company policy, right?"

"Of-of course I do, sir."

"Well then! Act like it. I want those write-ups on my desk for approval by the end of the day."

Mr. Bradshaw walks away from the rattled supervisor without saying another word. Cleo gives her an empathetic look before following him towards the elevators. He presses the "up" button once they reach it.

"I usually take the stairs, but something tells me you'd be more comfortable moving from floor to floor this way." Cleo tries not to get offended, but his tone is too nasty to ignore. They get inside of the elevator and the door closes.

"Excuse me?" She can't help but to ask. He turns to face her.

"Excuse you what?"

"The statement you just made… what did you mean by that?" He looks her up and down quickly.

"Well, it's no secret that you're toting a few extra pounds, and since I'm crunched for time, the elevator seems like a quicker option than waiting for you to climb the stairs-"

Cleo slaps the emergency stop button with her palm before he's able to finish his thought. The jerking halt catches Mr. Bradshaw off guard. Cleo steps into his personal space with tightly folded arms.

"Listen, I've taken just about enough of your shit! Yes, you're the boss, but that doesn't give you the right to talk down to people to make yourself feel better about your measly ass existence! I'm a great worker, but I'll be damned if I'm going to stand here and let you disrespect me or anyone else in my presence! I'd rather go back to my old job than to deal with this shit! As a matter of fact, that's exactly what I'm going to do; I quit!"

***

"... And then I popped out the emergency stop, got off on the main floor, and walked out of the building. He didn't say a word to me after I went off on him."

Cleo holds the phone in awkward silence. She nibbles at her lip nervously, "Pedra, are you mad?"

Pedra sighs, "I mean, I am a little disappointed, but no, I'm not mad. I did want you to make more money, but I'm not going to lie, someone should have told Mr. Bradshaw off a long time ago. I'm sorta glad you did." She giggles, "Honestly, I knew you were going to snap on him. You're too intolerant to deal with someone like his ass. It was doomed before it even started. I still had to try, though." Cleo humps her shoulders as if Pedra can see her.

"I don't know, Pedra. I just got so fucking mad! Like, who does he think he is bringing up my weight? He's a prick! He needs his ass kicked." Pedra giggles again.

"I agree. Too bad you won't be around to give him more tastes of his own medicine from time to time. He definitely needs someone to keep his ass in check." Cleo nods her head as if she agrees.

"Exactly! But now, I guess I'm sorta glad it's over. I will never have to see his unpleasant face again."

CHAPTER FIVE

"Good morning, Mr. Bernstein. I'm sorry I'm late. My badge didn't work at the front entrance." Cleo's old boss stares at her weirdly as she approaches him.

"Uh, good morning, Cleopatra. Your badge doesn't access this facility because you don't work here anymore." Cleo makes a confused face.

"But, I canceled my transfer request yesterday. Didn't you receive it?"

"I did, but then I got an email from a Mr. Bradshaw stating that he was hiring you to be his personal assistant and that you were reporting to him starting today. You didn't know that?" The perplexity on Cleo's face grows tenfold.

"I'm sorry, did you say Mr. Bradshaw's personal assistant?"

"Yeah. And I'm not going to lie, I'm a little jealous. When I saw your starting salary was 100k, I gasped. Congratulations, lady. You officially make more money than me now."

***

"What the hell is going on, Bradshaw?" Cleo doesn't hesitate to ask as soon as she barges in his office. He stands to his feet once he sees her.

"Good morning, Ms. Strong." She holds her hand up to silence him.

"Don't good morning me! I thought I was clear. I don't want to work for you."

Mr. Bradshaw stares at her without saying a word. Her hands press firmly against her hips in an impatient manner. Mr. Bradshaw takes her body in slowly.

"I thought the six figures would've changed your mind." She rolls her eyes at him.

"I know this may be too hard for you to understand, but money isn't everything, especially when someone has to work for an asshole like you."

He grabs his chest near his heart as if she punctured it, "Ouch! That was harsh." He smiles afterwards, revealing his humane side for the first time since she first encountered him. His perfect teeth throw her off slightly. She instantly shakes the feeling away.

"Listen, I know I can be difficult sometimes, but I feel like it's necessary. People will run all over you if you're too soft." Cleo refuses to respond to his words. He walks around his desk to join her, "Ms. Strong, just give me a chance to show you that I'm not all bad. There are good qualities about me, too. You'll also learn a lot, make a lot, and hopefully, you'll be sitting at the executive table for a meeting with the CEO one day. You have all of the characteristics needed to make a great management professional." Cleo looks lost by his drastic change in personality.

"I don't understand. Why are you going out of your way to convince me to work for you," she has to know. He steps closer to her, putting their bodies dangerously close to each other. Her breathing reacts to the smell of his masculine cologne. He looks down in her eyes.

"It's just something about you, Ms. Strong. I can't quite put my finger on it. It's something about you that is dominant, enduring, and necessary. You have this demeanor about you that this company needs," he licks his lips, "And I'm almost sure I need it, too."

***

"Stop fucking lying! He did not say that?!" Cleo fights the urge to smile during her and Pedra's lunch date. She looks around the huge cafeteria to make sure no one else is listening.

"He did. He said he needs whatever it is he thinks I have… whatever that means."

"But in what context did he say it?" Pedra pries. Cleo listens to the question, secretly shuttering at the memory of Mr. Bradshaw licking his juicy lips with his words.

"Professional, of course," she lies. Pedra shakes her head as if she can tell.

"Mmhmm… whatever. You're full of shit, but I'll let it slide." Cleo giggles.

The ladies get quiet while they tend to their different lunches. Pedra takes a bite of her burger while Cleo plays with her salad leaves. Pedra sips from her carbonated drink.

"So, did he tell you if you were getting your own desk or not?" Cleo pauses at Pedra's question. *She forgot to tell her about her new position!*

"Actually, yes. I already have it." Pedra's eyes get big at the news.

"Really? That's so cool! Congratulations, girl, and welcome to the team! I knew you could do it!"

"Thanks," Cleo says proudly.

"You said you already have it? Where? I didn't see you on the analyst floor this morning." Cleo hesitates with a response. She's not sure how Pedra is going to act once she finds out she passed her up in pay. She takes a deep breath before answering her question.

"Umm, well actually, I'm no longer an analyst. I'm actually Mr. Bradshaw's assistant now." Pedra spits out her drink at the news.

"His what?!" She inquires loudly. The ladies draw a small crowd from the other workers sitting near them. Cleo gets embarrassed.

"Pedra, really?" Pedra looks around at all of the newly tuned-in eyes.

"My bad, girl. I'm just… I'm a little shocked, that's all."

"Why is that so shocking?"

"Because, Mr. Bradshaw has never had an assistant! I don't even think that's a real position! It sounds like he made that shit up."

Cleo wants to respond to her friend, but Pedra's uninviting voice makes Cleo uninterested in engaging with her any further. Pedra tries to fix her tone as soon as she notices its unpleasantness, "But, it sounds like he wants to work closely with you, and he is very knowledgeable, so I guess that's a good thing. Besides, I'm sure he's compensating you heavily to deal with an asshole like him." Pedra chuckles after her statement, but Cleo doesn't crack a smile. Pedra's face changes immediately, "Oh my God… he is, isn't he? How much?"

Cleo makes an uneasy face. She leans in closely to whisper her next words, "$100,000."

CHAPTER SIX

Cleo tries her best to arrange the few items on her new desk, but her mind is too scrambled to concentrate on the elementary task. After she spilled the beans to Pedra about her new salary, Pedra's whole attitude towards her changed. She tried to act happy for Cleo, but the jealousy oozing from her glares were so uncomfortable that Cleo ended their lunch date early. Now, Cleo is sitting at her workstation in a huge space that is exclusively occupied by her and Mr. Bradshaw. The only thing that separates them is a partial wall divider with his desk sitting on the other side of it. She sighs at the thought of being alone with him all day. With how things went between them the last time, she's afraid their heads may bump again soon, and with a six-figure gig on the line, she can't afford things to go sour between her and him.

"Ms. Strong, I didn't expect to see you here already. I thought I was the only person that came back from lunch early," Mr. Bradshaw says as soon as he opens his office door. They lock eyes until he disappears behind the wooden divider. She hears him fiddling with something and then sitting down in his desk chair. She takes a deep breath before getting up and knocking on her side of the small wall.

Mr. Bradshaw chuckles as soon as she turns the corner, "No need to request permission to enter. We share an office for a reason. I want you to hear and see everything I do. You can't be a good assistant without us having a transparent relationship."

"Really? But what about intimate matters? I'm sure the conversations you have with your wife are private-"

"I don't have a wife," Mr. Bradshaw corrects her quickly. She immediately changes her wording.

"Girlfriend, then."

"I don't have one of those, either."

"Oh," Cleo says, feeling awkward about her wrong assumptions. Mr. Bradshaw smiles at her timid expression.

"You walked over here like you wanted to talk, so what's on your mind?" Mr. Bradshaw helps her jog her memory to her original inquiry. She secretly thanks him for saving her from the awkward moment.

"Well, I was wondering, what happened to your last assistant?" Mr. Bradshaw sits back in his chair as if Cleo asked an interesting question.

"My last assistant?"

"Yes. The one before me. What happened to him or her? You seem to be without one, so I was wondering what happened to them-"

"I'm not without one. I have you, don't I?" Cleo smacks her lips at his answer. He acts entertained by her annoyance, "I'm only joking. The truth is, I've never had one before you." Cleo looks shocked. *So, Pedra was right.*

"Seriously? But that big desk over there is for an assistant, right?"

"It is, but I never saw the need for one; Not until I met you, that is." Cleo has the urge to blush, but she successfully fights the feeling to do so. She clears her throat instead.

"Well, I don't know what I did to make you want me for the job, but I hope I don't disappoint you."
He sits up with his next words, "Ms. Strong, I don't think you could disappoint me if you tried."

***

Cleo stares at her laptop screen while clutching a glass of red wine in her hand. She searches the internet for "Mr. Bradshaw of Vella Industries" but gets the message "no results found" every time she hits enter.

"Damn," she mumbles before closing the computer. She tosses it to the couch cushion next to her. She doesn't know why, but she suddenly has a strong interest in Mr. Bradshaw's private life: His past, his social media accounts, *his sexual orientation…*
Honestly, she's having a very hard time believing that a man as handsome and successful as Mr. Bradshaw is single.
"Either he's gay, or he's lying about being in a relationship; And if he is single, his flaws must be overwhelmingly unbearable."

She shrugs off her concerns after realizing that he's just as mysterious as he is fine. Why is she so worried about his personal business, anyway? He's her boss, not her love interest.

Determined to fall asleep in her bed this evening, she retires to her room early. She sits her glass of wine down on her dark-colored nightstand to prepare for her slumber. She stares in the direction of her modest closet housing her small wardrobe. She walks over to it.
"Maybe I should dress up tomorrow," she considers, daydreaming about Mr. Bradshaw's eyes lighting up once he sees her actually putting forth effort into her appearance. She used to love wearing skirt suits and heels to work, but somewhere down the line, something sort of… changed.

Work turned into more of a task and less of a place to look nice. She dressed just professionally enough to get by, but now, her role has changed. She's no longer a customer service robot; she will officially be following one of the biggest names in the company. She has to look good on his Armani-covered side.

She pulls out a beautiful, red pencil skirt and blazer set. She smiles at the subtle sexiness of it. She lays it across her vanity chair and then takes a step back to admire it.

"That's the one," she says aloud, "That's the outfit that represents the first day of the rest of my life."

CHAPTER SEVEN

"Good morning, Tava."

Cleo hears Mr. Bradshaw greet his secretary as soon as he steps off of the elevator. Cleo stands to her feet when he enters their office.

"Good-" he begins to say before suddenly falling speechless. His jaw hits the floor when his eyes take in a stunning Cleopatra. She blushes at his reaction to her upgraded look.

"Good morning, Mr. Bradshaw," she says sweetly.

He struggles to find his words, "Wow. Good morning, Ms. Strong."

He proceeds out of her eyesight to lay his briefcase on his desk. He reappears a few seconds later.

"You're here early," he says with a smile. He acts like he wants to start a conversation just to get another look at her beauty. She nods her head.

"Of course I am. You did say we were stealing if we weren't actively working at our start time, so, here I am."

His eyes search her body lustfully, "You're right. Here you are."

His sudden hint of desire makes things awkward between them. Cleo looks away shyly, "So, what's on the agenda for today, Mr. Bradshaw?"

"Mr. Bradshaw? You're my assistant now. We're professional best friends, so it's only right that you call me by my first name." Cleo giggles.

"Is that right? Well, what's your first name, then?"

"You have to promise me you won't laugh." Cleo giggles again.

"I can't promise you that; Sorry." He chuckles, too.

"Alright— well, my name is Royal. Royal Bradshaw." Cleo's eyes react to the information.

"That is so funny-"

"I told you it would be."

"No, not funny like ha-ha, but funny like ironic. Your name is Royal, and my name comes from royalty; I'm Cleopatra." Royal nods his head as if he knows that already.

"I'm aware. Your paperwork was on my desk when you first got here, remember?"

"Duh! Of course," she mumbles embarrassingly. He steps closer to her.

"... And I'm glad you spotted those similarities, because that was the first thing I thought when I saw yours, too. We both have powerful names. What are the odds?" He gazes into her eyes like the answer to his question lies in the depths of her soul. The overwhelming connection makes Cleo flee to her seat.

"I don't know— one in a million, I guess." She aimlessly fumbles with the items on her desk. Royal smirks at her nervous actions.

"One in a million, huh? That was my guess, too."

***

"...And at the start of every day, I need this sheet right here to complete the paperwork that I must submit by noon." Royal points to the document on his desk, and then to the file on his computer. Cleo stands up straight after leaning over his shoulder for nearly 30 minutes. She's trying her best to follow his words, but her feet are starting to hurt so badly that the only thing she can think about is sitting down. She makes a pained face. Royal looks up at her.

"Is everything OK, Cleopatra?" Her ankles buckle while she attempts to straighten her posture.

"Yup. Everything is fine," she lies. He slides his chair back to get a better look at her. He glances down at the red pumps that are nearly crippling her.

"Your feet are hurting, aren't they?" Cleo doesn't want to seem like a wimp, so she tries to play it off.

"A little, but I'm fine." Royal gets up and proceeds to the other side of the divider. Cleo hears her desk chair being wheeled across the floor. She spots her boss guiding it around the corner.

He eases the chair behind her, "Have a seat."

"Thank you," she says before hesitating to sit down. She lets out a huge sigh of relief once her feet get a break. He grins.

"You must really be in pain. Why are you torturing yourself by wearing those things?"

"Because they go with my outfit," she jokes. He agrees as he sits down as well.

"You're right, they do." He slides closer to her, "You know, before I got into this type of work, I used to be a certified massage therapist."

"Seriously?" Cleo asks. He nods his head yes.

"I'm not certified anymore of course, but I'd like to think that I'm still pretty good with my hands." He glances down at her throbbing feet. Cleo instantly shakes her head no.

"Oh no, Mr. Bradshaw! You don't have to do that-" "I told you to call me Royal." He slides his hand down her right calf and lifts her foot towards his lap, "And don't worry about it. I insist."

Cleo tenses up while he slides her size 10 pump off of her stocking-covered foot. He sits the shoe on the floor next to him. "Try to relax, Cleopatra. As your new professional best friend, if I see you struggling with something that I can help you with, then I'm going to do just that. And as your new boss, the day has just begun. We have a long day of walking ahead of us, so I can't have you out of commission before we even start." Cleo blushes hard at Royal's words before he uses his thumbs to apply pressure to her foot. A tingling sensation travels up her leg as soon as he hits a nerve. She tries her best not to moan, even though his manly hands feel amazing. He reads the pleasure on her nearly silent face.

"Did you know there's over 7,000 nerve endings in each foot? I can pretty much tend to any part of your body by applying pressure to your feet."

"No, I don't think I knew that," Cleo tries to respond in a normal voice. She closes her eyes because of the state of euphoria he's putting her body in.

"Really? Well, let me show you."

Royal slides his strong hands towards her toes. He skillfully massages them in firm, circular motions.

"Oh! I can feel a sensation in my face! That's crazy!" Cleo exclaims shockingly. Royal smiles at her reaction.

"What about this?" He moves his attention to her heel. She jerks from the random twinge in her lower back.

"What the…?" He chuckles. "I'm not going to lie to you Royal, this is weird."

"You think that's weird, then wait until you feel this."

He slides his thumbs along the outside of her foot, creating that tingly feeling that moves up her leg again. The sensation travels upward until it shoots through her thigh and heads straight for her vagina. She gasps as soon as she notices it. Her clit wakes up from the sudden jolt of energy. Royal watches her reaction like a hawk. She makes eye contact with him when his hands develop a sensual rhythm. She's not sure how he's doing it, but it almost feels like he's fucking her. Her leg shivers just like they would if his dick was inside of her. He bites his lip at the thought of penetrating her without actually doing so.

"Sorry to interrupt, Mr. Bradshaw," Tava says as soon as she opens the office door. She stops in her tracks once she sees Cleo's foot wedged in Royal's hands. Cleo tries to remove it from his clutches, but he refuses to let it go. She covers her face embarrassingly as a second option.

He tightens his jaw in his secretary's direction, "Tava, I've asked you several times not to barge in my office without permission."

She stutters, "I- I apologize Mr. Bradshaw, but this is urgent. Mr. Collins called and told me to give you a message." She hesitates before walking towards Royal. He drops Cleo's foot in his lap to grab the small slip from Tava. He reads over it quickly.

"Thank you," he states in a dismissive tone. She scurries away without saying another word. He looks at Cleo, "Mr. Collins is the CEO of Vella industries. Apparently, I've been doing such great work that he wants to fly down to meet me. This will be the first time I've ever seen the guy. He'll be here at the end of next week."

CHAPTER EIGHT

Cleo stares at the time on her cellphone change from 11:59 to 12:00. She sighs at the thought of eating lunch with a funny-acting Pedra in the building's cafeteria. She hasn't talked to her since their strangely negative conversation yesterday, and honestly, she's not up for the task of being uncomfortable just to grab a bite to eat.

"Fuck lunch today," she thinks to herself, *"I'll just eat when I get home."*

Royal finishes up the last of his midday paperwork and submits the documents to the higher-ups. *"Just in time for lunch,"* he thinks after glancing at the time on his computer. He watches the divider closely, expecting to see Cleo emerge from behind it at any second. He speaks up once the time changes to 12:01.

"Cleopatra? Are you going to lunch?" He exclaims in the direction of her desk.

"No. I decided to wait until I get home to eat."

Royal stands up curiously and walks until they're in each other's view, "Wait until you get home? Why?"

"Umm, intermittent fasting," she thinks up quickly, "I'm only allowed to eat four hours a day, so I eat when I get home." Royal smacks his lips at her lie.

"And when did you start that? Because I've seen you in the cafeteria eating lunch with your analyst friend several times."

She makes a caught face, and then a confused one, "You've seen me eating in the lunchroom? I didn't know you ate lunch with us."

"I don't, but that doesn't mean I don't know what's going on in there." He makes a face like he's lying this time. Cleo lets it slide, "So, I know this intermittent eating thing is something that you're either A. Making up, or B. Just came up with in the past day or two."

Cleo opens her mouth to respond, but no words come out. Royal sits on top of her desk, "Look, I'm really sorry if I made you feel a certain way when I brought up your weight. I was wrong and out of line. I had no business being that rude to you, so I apologize."

She humps her shoulders, "It's OK. It's not like you were lying. It would have taken me a longer time than you to climb the stairs. Thanks for using the elevator today, by the way. You saved me a ton of embarrassment." Cleo laughs, but Royal doesn't. He stares at her so seriously that it halts her chuckling.

"You should never feel embarrassed, especially about something as juvenile as that. You're beautiful, Cleopatra, and never let me, or any other asshole, make you feel differently."

***

"Wow! This is where you eat lunch every day? This place looks expensive," Cleo exclaims once her and Royal walk through the doors of one of the most lavish restaurants she's ever stepped foot in. They stop at the greeter's podium.

"Absolutely not. I'm just trying to impress you," he says with a smile. Cleo can't help but to smile back.

"Ahh, Mr. Bradshaw; Would you like your usual table?"

"That'll be fine, Barrett," he answers, allowing the young host to show them to a cozy table near a window. Cleo smacks her lips at him once they take their seats.

"You don't come here every day, huh?" Royal displays a guilty grin.

"Not every day, but maybe once or twice a week." They both seem amused by his comment.

"Really Royal, you didn't have to do this. I told you I could've eaten when I got home. It was no biggie."

"Nonsense, Cleopatra. We still have several hours of work left and I can't have you assisting me on an empty stomach. Eat now. I insist. It's my treat."

"Well, since you put it that way," Cleo picks up the menu and stares at it, "What's the most expensive thing in this joint?"

Royal smirks, "You better be careful, woman. Anything over 50 bucks and this is a date."

She glances at him from over the top of her menu, "50 bucks? Cheap date."

He licks his lips while engaging with her, "That's the average price of an appetizer here. You're definitely going to go over $50. I just wanted you to know what you're getting yourself into. You've been warned."

***

Cleo and Royal giggle the entire elevator ride and the walk towards their workspace. His secretary watches them in shock as they happily move past her. They make it inside of the office and close the door.

"I can't believe your bill came up to $49.50. You are something else, you know that?"

"I know, but I had to make that Grant work for me. I don't go on dates unless a guy properly asks me out on one." Royal grins at her words.

"Understood." He walks towards his chair.

"Tava looked completely thrown off by us walking in together like that."

Royal removes his suit jacket for the first time ever and hangs it on the back of his chair. Cleo swallows hard at the sight of his chiseled upper body bulging noticeably through his dress shirt. He loosens the knot on his silk tie. Cleo tries not to stare, but the visual is too damn good to turn away from. He purposely ignores her lustful glares.

"It wasn't us walking in together that threw her off, it was me laughing. I don't think I've ever smiled in front of her; Not once."

"But why not? You have a great smile. And besides, people would like you more if-"

"I don't care if people like me or not. We're all here to do a job. We don't have to be friendly for that."

Royal uses a nasty tone with Cleo. She takes a startled step back.

"Understood," she says, promptly moving to her side of the office. Royal sighs before following her.

"Cleopatra, I didn't mean me and you, I meant me and everyone else."

"But I work here just like everyone else, so I shouldn't be treated any differently. That's only fair, Royal. Oh, I'm sorry, I meant Mr. Bradshaw."

CHAPTER NINE

"So, that's how it is now, huh?"

Cleo turns her nightstand lamp on as soon as she answers the phone for Pedra. She clears the sleep from her throat.

"Pedra, what are you talking about?"

"I haven't heard from you since lunchtime yesterday. And then, I wait for you in the lunchroom today just for you to stand me up."

Cleo stares at the time on her digital alarm clock: *10:03pm.*

"I'm sorry, girl. Things were hectic today-"

"Oh believe me, I've heard." Cleo sits up slightly from her pillow.

"What do you mean by that?"

"I mean I ran into Tava at the end of the day and she filled me in on all of the juicy gossip involving you and our boss."

"Juicy gossip? What juicy gossip?" Cleo asks quickly.

"Well, I heard that Mr. Bradshaw was giving you foot rubs in the office; And then, I heard he took you out of the building for lunch."

Cleo covers her face in shame as if someone can see her. She takes a deep breath, "That is what happened, but it's not what you think-"

"Save it. You know what? I can't believe I thought we were friends! I jumped through all of those hoops to get you to the new building just for you to use me as a disposable stepping stool! I mean, I want you to advance and all, but I at least thought we'd still be friends during the climb! I should've known better, though. You haven't had a man in so long that you can't tell the difference between a good choice and a bad choice!"

Cleo looks taken aback, "You know what, Pedra, fuck you! If it's not you with the good job or the boyfriend, then you always have something negative to say about it! You're full of shit!"

"No, you are! This guy just called you a fat ass a couple of days ago and now you're sniffing behind him like a lost puppy! How pathetic are you?"

"You know what? I don't need this," Cleo says before hanging up in Pedra's face. She slams her head into her pillow, allowing her newfound anger to consume her. Tears form in her eyes, but she refuses to let one fall. She's officially over everyone and their bullshit. The only thing she's going to be concerned with from here on out is her motherfucking money. *Fuck relationships.*

***

"Good morning, Mr. Bradshaw. I took the liberty of requesting your morning documents already. They should be coming out of the printer as we speak." Royal pauses in his tracks to listen to Cleo. He looks impressed.

"Wow. Thanks, Cleopatra." He glances at his watch, "You got all of that done before 8:00? That's magnificent work."

Cleo barely smiles at the compliment. She takes a seat at her desk, "Let me know if there's anything else I can help you with, sir."

Royal has the urge to talk to her about what happened between them yesterday but decides now is not the right time. He nods his head at her instead. He slowly proceeds to his desk.

"So, how was your night?" He asks, trying to throw her a line to see if she'll bite.

"It was fine, thanks," she says in a professional, but dry manner. Royal sighs. *He can't help himself.*

"Cleopatra, I'm sorry."

"No need to be, Mr. Bradshaw. Like you said, we don't need to be friendly to do our jobs, and I totally agree." He walks towards her desk.

"Well don't. That was bullshit. If you would've asked me about my night, then I would've told you that I spent it thinking about us." Cleo's eyes light up unwillingly.

"Us?"

"Yes— us. Cleopatra, I had a really good time kicking it with you yesterday. I forgot how great it felt to chat and laugh with someone without having so many defense mechanisms in play. Look, I was wrong, and I apologize. It's just hard for me to open up to people. I haven't done that in a very long time." Cleo smiles.

"It's perfectly fine, Mr. Bradshaw. No harm, no foul-"

"Can you please go back to calling me Royal? Every time you call me Mr. Bradshaw, I cringe for some reason. I don't know why, but when you say it, it sounds like I'm in trouble or something." Cleo giggles.

"Maybe because you are."

***

"Damn. It's already lunch time, Cleopatra." She looks over at her boss that she's been working next to at his desk.

"I know. I've been looking forward to it. If I look at one more document, I'm going to scream." Royal sits back in his seat with his pen against his lips like he's thinking. He places it on the table.

"How about we get out of here?"

"You mean, eat lunch together again? I'm telling you, Royal, that $50 won't work for me two days in a row. I only pulled it off yesterday because I wanted to prove a point." He smirks.

"You won't have to worry about that. I'll cook us something." Cleo looks at him weirdly.

"What do you mean 'you'll cook us something'? You want us to go to your place?" Royal leans towards Cleo to make their conversation more intimate.

"I was thinking, we could take the rest of the day off; Eat, chill, watch movies. We got a day's worth of work done before noon, so according to company policy, our workday is complete. We're salary employees, Cleopatra. We technically have no start and end times. As long as the work is done, we're free to leave."

"But what if someone needs you?"

"Then I'll tell Tava to take a message because I'll be out of the office for the remainder of the day, and if it's a real emergency, then she can call my cell." Cleo makes an unsure face.

"I don't know about this, Royal."

"Why? Are you afraid I'll bite?" He licks his lips after the question. Cleo's heartbeat reacts to the sexy gesture.

"Royal— I—," she's not sure what to say. He moves his face closer to hers, staring strongly into her eyes. Her breathing picks up from the intense moment. He gives her a half grin.

"Trust me, Cleopatra. I'm not going to do anything that you don't want me to do."

Cleo swallows hard after his statement. *That's what she's afraid of.*

CHAPTER TEN

"Wow," Cleo mumbles when they step inside of Royal's secluded house on the hill. He walks in after her and closes the door.

"It's a little small, but it'll do." She smacks her lips at his facetious statement.

"Oh, please! What is this? A six bedroom, eight bath?"

"No, it's a four bedroom, six bath, thank you very much." She playfully nudges him in the arm. He chuckles as he removes his shoes, "Pearl marble and white carpet; Wearing shoes in the house is a huge pet peeve of mine." She takes his words as a warning and kicks off her heels, too. He drops his briefcase near the front door, "Come on. Let me show you around."

"Sheesh, this place is massive," Cleo points out while they make their way through the immaculately clean rooms on the first floor. Everything is so neat and in order that she's afraid to touch anything. He walks her towards the kitchen.

"I guess it doesn't seem that way to me because I hardly ever visit these rooms. Besides the maid giving them a light cleaning once a month, that's the only time anyone steps foot in them."

"The maid, huh?" Cleo asks while shaking her head in disbelief. Royal glances at her but doesn't answer her question.

Royal opens up his massive, stainless-steel refrigerator as Cleo takes a seat at his long kitchen island.

She rubs her hands across the cool, pearl marble countertop before looking in his direction.

"So, why do you have a house so big when it's just you? This is definitely a family home." Royal takes an uncomfortable deep breath because of the nature of Cleo's question. Even though he's usually guarded, he decides to answer it for her.

"When I moved into this house, I had every intention of having a family— a huge one. My fiancé moved in with me." Cleo's eyes can't help but to react to the news. He shakes his head to ease her mind.

"No, I'm not with her anymore. We broke up years ago. It was painful, messy, but necessary. She ended up cheating on me because I was 'never around'. I guess that's what happens when you work as much as I do."

Cleo can tell Royal is trying his best to fight off those old, painful feelings. She jumps up from her seat.

"Hey, it's lunch time, remember? But all I see you pulling out is breakfast food." She stands near the refrigerator with him. "How about I find something to make us and you grab the wine? We're going to need it."

He smiles at her for secretly trying to save him from his hurtful past, "Oh, so you think you can cook better than me, huh?" She places her hand on her hips.

"Oh, please! What do you think? I'm this big by accident? No, sweetie! Your professional best friend can throw down. Just watch me work."

***

"Damn, Cleopatra. That was so fucking good," Royal blurts out after taking the last bite of his marinated chicken Caesar salad with homemade dressing and croutons." She smiles.

"Thank you. I told you I could throw down. I'm just glad you had all of the ingredients I needed to pull this off."

He gives her an interested look before sipping the Pinot Noir from his glass.

"That, you did. So tell me, with all of your desirable characteristics, why are you single?" Cleo becomes instantly embarrassed by the question. She decides to respond with a smart remark.

"Who said I was single?"

Royal gawks at her, resembling that of a hungry beast that just spotted his prey. He refuses to give her clever reply any attention. She awkwardly plays with the stem of her glass, "I don't know. I've always had trouble with dating. I'm starting to think it's not for me."

"How can you say that? Dating is for everyone when it's with the right person."

"I'm not sure if I believe in that, either." She finally looks into Royal's piercing eyes. He tightens his well-defined jaw.

"I'm really sorry you feel that way, but you should never give up on the possibility of meeting the one for you. You never know, the answer could be right before your eyes."

Cleo stares at him and he at her. She finally breaks their engaging glares before her eyes tell him something she doesn't want him to know.

"You're asking me why I'm single, but what about you?" Cleo turns the tables as she takes a big gulp from her glass.

"I told you, I had someone, but it didn't work."

"And you also said that was years ago. You haven't deemed it necessary to move on by now?" He sighs loudly.

"I do want to move on, but I'm in no rush to do so. You have to be careful with strangers nowadays. Their intentions can be sinister."

"Sounds like you have trust issues."

"I do, indeed. I told you I got my heart ripped out by the woman I was supposed to marry. Wouldn't you have trust issues, too?"

Cleo turns her sights away from the very touchy conversation. She glances towards a huge TV and creme leather sofa behind her.

"No dining room setup?" She asks without looking at him. He picks up his glass as he stands to his feet. He grabs her arm on the way past her. She hurries and snatches her drink before he's able to tug her away from the kitchen island. They move towards the couch to sit down.

"Why have a dining room table when I usually eat alone?" He cuts the television on but neither him, nor Cleo, looks in its direction.

"Well, you didn't eat alone today." Royal turns his body towards hers.

"You're right. I didn't."

He divides his attention between her eyes and her lips. The tension from the moment has Cleo's heart about to beat out of her chest. His lips move towards hers. She speaks before he's able to kiss her.

"What about that movie? You said we would eat, chill, and watch movies, didn't you?" He pauses his movements before smiling at her attempt to extinguish the fire burning between them. He gives her some space.

"You're right, I did say that." He grabs the remote again, "So, what do you want to watch?"

CHAPTER ELEVEN

"I can't believe you've never seen *Black Panther* before! You can't be black," Cleo teases as soon as the movie's end credits roll. Royal swallows the last of his fourth glass of wine before responding.

"I told you, I don't watch much TV… or drink, for that matter," he says, placing the empty glass on the table.

Cleo sets down her empty glass as well. "I drink, but not this type of wine. Shit Royal, I think I'm buzzing." He glances back at the two empty bottles on the kitchen island. Cleo lays her head back and closes her eyes. Royal turns his attention towards her.

"You know what else I haven't done in a while?"

"No, what?" She asks without moving her eyelids.

"Take a nap. Life is always so hectic that I can't remember the last time I climbed in my bed in the middle of the day and went to sleep."

"Mmhmm," she hums. He rubs her hand, causing her to look in his direction.

"We should take a nap." Cleo sits up as a reaction to his words. She immediately tries to stop the room from spinning.

"No, I'm good," she lies.

"You're not good. And you'd be sadly mistaken if you think I'm going to allow you to drive away from my place in the condition you're in." She stares at his serious face and realizes that his stance can't be persuaded. She sighs in defeat.

"Alright, fine. I can nap right here on the couch."

Royal makes an annoyed sound before standing up, "Woman, didn't I just say I had four bedrooms?" He holds out his hands for a drunken Cleo. He tugs her up once she grabs them. "Come on. I'll show you where you're sleeping."

Cleo sluggishly follows a surprisingly well-coordinated Royal up his grand staircase. He moves down a long hallway.

"You'll be in the bedroom next to mine." He turns the corner with his words. Cleo pauses when she spots the gorgeous gold and white trim dominating the elegant space. He points to a door on the right wall.

"That's the bathroom. The master suite is on the other side of it. It's a shared space." He turns to look at her, "Any questions?" She shakes her head no, "Good. I'm going to sleep."

He begins loosening his tie before he makes it out of the room. He closes the door behind him. Cleo faces the beautiful bed with impressed eyes. *She's about to have some of the best sleep she's had in a while...*

Except that's not true. Cleo is having the hardest time falling asleep. She tosses and turns on the soft sleeper until she's unable to take it anymore.

"I can't sleep in this suit," she mutters while looking down at the navy-blue skirt set. She glances in the direction of the closed bedroom door, and then the closed bathroom door. She removes her clothes after she double checks her privacy.

Cleo climbs underneath the Egyptian cotton comforter wearing only her bra and panties. She cuddles up underneath the cover. She closes her eyes to drift off to sleep but opens them quickly when her mind daydreams about Royal coming in the room and getting in the bed with her. She shakes the thought away quickly. *"Royal is my boss. He's off limits."*

***

"Cleopatra?... Cleo?" Royal says when he slowly opens the bedroom door. The darkness of its interior makes it hard for him to see any of her facial features. Even though he's trying to wake her, he still tiptoes towards the side of the bed. His shirtless body stands over the peaceful view of her slumber.

He marvels at the sight of her juicy body lying motionless in his guest bed. He slowly slides the cover off of her top half, exposing her size H breasts. He licks his lips at the sight of her lacy, black bra.

"Cleo?" He mumbles again. She still doesn't respond to his faint calls. He eases down softly next to her.

"Cleopatra?" He calls her name louder this time, mainly because he needs her awake to stop him from doing the sexual things he so desperately wants to do to her body. She finally opens her eyes.

"Royal? What time is it?" She asks after looking around the nearly pitch-black room. She sits up slightly but covers up once she notices her boobs are out. His mouth salivates at the thought of placing her nipples between his lips.

"It's after 9:00. I was just coming in here to let you know dinner is ready if you want to eat."

"9:00! Dammit, Royal! I slept the whole damn day away!"

"Yeah. You and me, both. I guess we really needed the rest." He stands to his feet, creating the sexiest silhouette Cleo has ever seen. The light from the hallway outlines his body in a way that captures the godliness of his being. He walks over to the closet and grabs a t-shirt from a hanger.

"I have an oversized tee if you want to wear it instead of your work clothes." His gorgeous body moves towards Cleo. Her pussy wakes up when he enters her personal space. He sits on the bed and hands it to her. She hesitates before grabbing it.

"What about bottoms?"

"What about them?"

"Well, you gave me a shirt, but no pants." He nods his head.

"Yeah— it's a pretty long shirt."

"On you, maybe. But on me… probably not." He makes an uneasy face.

"I can give you a pair of basketball shorts, but I'd have to find them first. Just put on the shirt for now. Trust me. It won't look as bad as you think."

CHAPTER TWELVE

"Mm, that smells so good," Cleo says as she enters the kitchen to join Royal. He's sitting both plates of food down on the island when she comes into view. He stops all motion to gawk at her in a starstruck fashion. She stops in her tracks once she reads the look on his face, "Is everything alright?"

He swallows at the sight of her thick body rocking the fuck out of his old shirt. He finally rests the plates down on the counter, "Yes, everything is fine."

"You sure?" She asks, tugging at the tee, which falls just below her ass cheeks. He nods his head yes.

"If things weren't good before, they're definitely perfect now." She blushes.

"Stop it, Royal. You're always trying to flirt with me."

"Trying?" He inquires, sitting down in the seat beside her. His leg rests against hers, causing sparks to shoot through her entire body. She tries to ignore them.

"Yes, trying— because we both know we can't go there. You're my boss, remember?"

"I'm well aware of our positions, but that shouldn't have anything to do with us personally."

"But it does, though. What if we start dating and things go bad? We would still have to work together, unless you fired me, of course."

"*Or* things could go well, we'd get married, and you'd have my babies." His words make Cleo choke on the water she's drinking. He turns to face her, "I'm just saying,

Cleo. Where's the harm in trying?" He turns her chair around to face him as well. Her legs rest snugly between his. He places both of his hands on her meaty thighs. They slowly slide upward.

"Royal, why me?" He pauses.

"Why not you?"

"Well, you made fun of my weight when I first started working for you-"

"And I apologized for that. The truth is, I don't like skinny women, never have. When I saw you, I was so attracted to you that I didn't know what to do… so I put my damn foot in my mouth." He shakes his head at his stupid actions. Cleo makes an unsure face.

"Royal-"

"Cleo, I've never begged a woman for her affection before, and I don't plan on starting now. But please, consider the possibilities if you and I tried to see where this thing goes. Just think about it. Use your heart, not your mind."

He lets go of her legs before turning around to tend to his food. She stares at the side of his face for a moment before facing her dinner to do the same thing. She plays with the pasta on her plate instead of eating it. This situation between her and Royal has put her appetite on the back burner. He glances over and notices her off-putting demeanor.

"What's on your mind?"

"I'm just scared, Royal. I'm scared of what would happen if we actually acted on our impulses. What if it destroys us?"

"And what if it doesn't?" He counters in an impatient tone, "And if I acted on my impulses right now, I'd have you for dinner instead of this fucking linguini. You'd be sitting right where my plate is and I'd be slurping all over your pussy instead of this pasta."

The shock covering Cleo's face is indescribable. He nods his head to let her know that what she heard is correct, "That's right, I said what I said, and I meant that shit."

The cockiness in his voice awakens something within Cleo. She has the strong urge to call his bluff, but she knows by the look in his eyes he's not bluffing. Even though it's been forever since a man went down on her, she'd still be too shy to let her boss do it... *Although the thought of him putting his head between her legs is a major turn on.*

Cleo and Royal exchange intense stares. She can tell by his body language that if she gave him the green light, he'd pounce on her this very second. Trying to limit the growing sexual tension, she finally breaks their eye contact, "I can tell you meant it."

She retreats from the heated topic to take a bite of her food for the first time. She reacts to its awesome flavor as soon as it touches her tongue. She finishes chewing the linguini and shrimp before speaking, "Wow, Royal. This is really good."

He looks disappointed by the change of subject but doesn't voice that he is. "Thanks. I told you I can cook a little, too. We may need to hold a cook-off one evening or something."

Cleo takes another bite before responding to his challenge. "Sounds good to me. I don't mind kicking your butt."

"And I don't mind kissing yours."

"Royal!" Cleo exclaims before giggling at his words. He tries to direct her back to a subject he's dying to physically explore. She smacks her lips, "We should finish eating our food before it gets cold."

***

"Thanks for helping me clean the kitchen, Cleopatra. I really appreciate it." Cleo dries off the last plate he just handed her and places it in the cabinet.

"No problem. I did cook this afternoon, too. Besides, I can't leave your maid with a mess this big." Royal side-eyes her for her facetious remark.

"You shouldn't worry about it. She gets paid very well for her services."

"I'm sure she does." Cleo faces Royal, "Well, it's late. I think I should head home now." Royal checks the time on his stainless-steel range.

"It's close to midnight. Maybe you should stay here tonight." Cleo immediately disagrees.

"I can't stay over, Royal."

"And why can't you?" He steps closer to her. She places her hand on her hip.

"You know why."

"No, I have absolutely no idea why."

"Well, for starters, I need to shower-"

"And I have a bathroom for that."

"...I need pajamas-"

"I have another shirt you can wear."

"...And I also need a change of undergarments and I need something to wear to work tomorrow-"

"Which I can have here for you by the time we head out for work. If you tell me your size, I can have the maid pick you up something on the way over here in the morning. Tomorrow is her cleaning day."

Royal seems to have an answer for everything. Cleo sighs, "Royal, am I really supposed to trust my fashion decisions to a woman I've never met before?"

"You should, because I do."

"But, what about our sleeping arrangements-"

"Look, Cleopatra. I'm not trying to force you into doing something you don't want to do, but I really don't think you should leave tonight. Not because I want you here, even though I do, but because driving down the hill we're on is dangerous, especially if you're unfamiliar with it. It's pitch-black dark out there and those twists and turns on that narrow road can be deadly. Please, just trust me. I don't want you getting hurt. Stay with me tonight. I insist."

CHAPTER THIRTEEN

"I can't believe I let him talk me into this," Cleo mumbles to herself as she prepares to take a shower in the bathroom that is shared by both her and Royal's bedrooms. She carries the towels he gave her towards its entrance. She knocks at the restroom door to make sure it isn't inhabited. Once she receives no response, she slowly opens it. She clicks the light on, revealing a room just as gorgeous and neatly kept as the rest of the house. It follows the same white and gold theme as the bedroom she's staying in, making her wonder if Royal's master suite possesses the same color scheme.

"Stop it, Cleo. You have no desire to see that man's bedroom," she lies to herself. She closes the door behind her and sets the towels on the space next to the 'his and hers' sinks. She turns around to face a type of stand-alone shower she's never seen before. It almost looks like a sauna because of its size, and the glass walls that's encapsulating it gives the shower-taker no privacy whatsoever.

She swings open the door and stares at an array of knobs. *She's going to need a manual to turn this damn shower on.*

She sighs annoyedly, "Royal! Could you come here for a second, please?" Cleo waits patiently for the door on Royal's side of the bathroom to open. Once it does, the sight of his shirtless body nearly chokes Cleopatra. She tries her best not to seem impressed, but the desire glaring from her eyes is too hard to hide. He approaches her with a heavy stride.

"I love the way you call my name. What's up, gorgeous?" She swallows down every urge she has to rub all over his perfect chest. She returns her attention to the complicated shower instead.

"I know this may be a stupid question, but how the hell do I work this thing?" He smiles sexily at her before reaching for the knobs.

"It's definitely not a stupid question. I had to watch a YouTube video to learn how to operate this damn shower." He twists a few of them and Cleo watches as each shower head comes on one by one. "I don't know how many streams of water you want, but I can make the water come from the walls, too."

"That won't be necessary. I just want to take an ordinary shower. Nothing special." He takes a step back once he turns off all of the sources of water but one. She thanks him.

"Let me know if you need me to wash your back or something." Cleo smacks her lips while playfully shoving Royal in the arm. He stumbles towards his room, "Have a good shower, Cleopatra."

***

Cleo wraps up in an oversized towel after taking one of the best showers she's taken in a while. At first, she kept worrying that Royal would bust in the bathroom on her, but after she made the conscious decision to not lock either door, she realized that she was secretly hoping he would. *He never did, though.*

She stares at herself in a mirror surrounded by such brilliant light that she sees every detail of her brown face. She stares at her nearly clear skin, *"I need to exfoliate."*

"Good. You're finally done," Royal says from behind Cleo. She turns around suddenly when she hears his voice. He walks towards the shower wearing only a towel wrapped low on his waist. Cleo's bottom jaw drops to the floor.

"Royal! What are you doing in here?" He looks at her after cutting on every single shower head in the shower.

"What does it look like I'm doing?" He responds in a smart tone. She looks away shyly.

"I'm sorry. It is late. I didn't realize I was taking so long."

"Hey, don't apologize. It's all good." He walks in her direction carrying a brand-new toothbrush, "I meant to give this to you earlier. I don't know if you brush your teeth before bed or not, but just in case you do, the toothpaste is right there."

He points to the tube near the sink closest to his bedroom's entrance. He returns to the shower right after his words.

Cleo watches his strong back muscles through the mirror. Her eyes grow three times their normal size once he lets the towel covering his lower half drop to the marble floor. His defined ass is the last thing she sees before he steps in the shower. He closes its door behind him.

"My God!" she shouts internally. She wants to leave to give him his privacy, but her feet refuse to move towards her bedroom door. Instead, they move in the toothpaste's direction. She picks it up without taking her eyes off of his reflection in the mirror. His naked body looks heavenly through the foggy glass walls of the shower. The water trickles down his chocolate skin ever so gracefully. *Damn... lucky water.*

Her lust-filled eyes dart away from him once he looks in her direction. She tries to act like she's busy brushing her teeth even though she has yet to remove the top from the minty toothpaste. She hears the shower door swing open, "Cleo, are you OK?"

"Yeah— Yes, I'm fine."

"Are you sure?" He double checks. Cleo glances at his reflection again, only to find him standing in its doorway with his huge dick dangling like a pendulum between his legs. The unbelievably erotic sight takes her breath away.

"Positive," she mumbles.

He smirks, "OK, just making sure." He steps back inside of the shower and closes the door. She finally applies the toothpaste to her toothbrush. *Let me get the hell out of here before I get myself in trouble.*

CHAPTER FOURTEEN

Cleo can't sleep, but it's not because she took a long nap earlier today. It's because she can't get Royal's sexy ass off of her mind. Every time she closes her eyes, his perfect, nude body is the only thing she sees. She can't believe he was that comfortable being naked in front of her, and his dick…
Let's just say her mouth hasn't stopped salivating since she saw it.

Cleo's body stiffens up once she notices that her bedroom door that leads to the bathroom is being opened. The creaking noise it makes sends chills down her spine. She quickly closes her eyes to pretend she's sleeping. She can feel Royal's presence moving towards her. She swallows the growing nervousness in her throat.

Without saying a word, Royal grabs the comforter draped over her t-shirt covered body. He slowly slides it down her breasts as if he's trying not to wake her. It inches down her chest, and then her stomach. She panics once it hits her waist after realizing she's not wearing any panties. She clinches it with her hands before her bare vagina is exposed.

"Royal, what are you trying to do?" She asks suddenly. She looks at him like she caught him doing something he had no business doing. His almost nude body shocks her once she takes in the sight of him. His boxers are the only things standing between her and his gorgeous cock.

"What does it look like I'm trying to do?" He responds, sounding just like he did earlier before his shower. He rests his manly body on his knees next to the bed. Cleo clutches the cover tighter.

"Royal, we can't do this-"

"Just let me see her. You saw mine, now I want to see yours."

"But I didn't ask to see it. You showed me-"

"Shh…" he states, placing his index finger over her moving lips. He uses the other hand to slide down her body and underneath the cover. Her legs tense up at the feel of his fingers nearing her pussy. She closes her thighs tightly.

"Once we do this, there's no going back." Royal stands to his feet with a sigh.

"You know what, you talk too much, woman." He carries his handsome being to the other side of the bed and climbs in it with her. She watches in amazement as he gets underneath the cover, too. "What about cuddling? Is that off limits as well?"

Cleo doesn't know what to say, so she says nothing at all. Royal reads her silence as an invitation. He takes her in his muscular arms without warning, causing goosebumps to instantly form on her skin. She tenses up at first, but eventually relaxes once the masculine smell of his deodorant enters her nose. She lays her head on his strong chest.

"Good night, Cleopatra." Royal whispers. His firm hold on her curves makes her feel desired and protected. She closes her eyes and lets the rhythm of his heartbeat soothe her.

"Good night, Royal."

***

"Size 14, right?" The older lady asks with a smile. Cleo nods her head awkwardly.

"Size 14," she repeats, taking the dark green suit from Royal's maid. Cleo admires its high-quality fabric once it exchanges between their hands. *This damn skirt set must've cost a fortune!*

"It's beautiful," Cleo mutters more to herself than the maid. The woman's smile never leaves her face.

"I thought so, too, when I saw it. With the way Royal described you, I thought it would be perfect for you." Cleo seems flattered.

"The way Royal described me?" The lady nods her head yes.

"He seems very fond of you."

The sweet woman hands Cleo an additional bag before stepping out of the bedroom that Cleo and Royal slept in last night. She turns around to lay the gorgeous suit on the bed. Royal appears in the bathroom doorway right after.

"Do you like it?" He asks with his dress shirt halfway buttoned. He sticks his hands in his slack pockets before leaning against the door frame. Cleo gestures that she does without looking his way.

"Royal, this is so beautiful, but it's too much. I'll pay you back whatever you spent on it."

"No need, " he replies, stepping towards her, "It's on me. I insist."

"You know, you're always insisting on something." She finally looks at an approaching Royal. He wraps his arms around her without her permission. He gazes into her eyes.

"I know, just like I insist on you letting me kiss you."

"Kiss me? No," Cleo instantly disagrees. Royal looks disappointed.

"You know the harder you resist, the harder I'm going to try, right?"

She smirks, "Is this coming from the same guy that said he's not chasing any woman?" He smiles.

"I'm not chasing any woman. I'm chasing *my* woman. You're already mine, you just don't know it yet." Royal plants a kiss on Cleo's forehead before she's able to process his words. He releases her and heads towards the bathroom.

"Your woman?" She asks in an unbelievable tone. He glances over his shoulder but decides to completely ignore the question.

"I also had her pick you up some underwear and hair care products. I know how hard it is to maintain natural hair. I had an afro in high school." She stares at the bag on the bed next to her new skirt set.

"Wow. Thank you, Royal. I can't believe she was able to get all of this stuff this early in the day."

"We have our ways. Now, get dressed. We don't want to be late for work."

CHAPTER FIFTEEN

Cleo stares at her TV, but she's not really watching it. She's been thinking about her boss since she left his side a few hours ago. She usually loves her small apartment, but now that she's been inside of a place as huge and lavish as Royal's home, she can't help but to want more. The confusing part is, she can't figure out if she wants more because she deserves it, or if she wants more because Royal has it; And if it is because of Royal, could it be that she wants to share his space with him instead of creating one of her own? She sips her wine to stop her mind from going there.

"DING!" Her text message alert goes off, which startles her. The only friend she has is Pedra, but they aren't talking right now. She sits up straight once she sees Royal's name.

"Hey, professional BFF. I'm not going to lie, you've been on my mind since we left work. I think I miss you."

Cleo smiles hard at the message. She thinks of 100 different responses, but decides on "Oh, really?" She impatiently waits for a reply, hoping hers wasn't too vague.

"Yes, really. What are you doing right now?"

She texts back as soon as she reads the message, "Watching a movie with a glass of wine in my hand. What about you?"

"I'm sitting in your parking lot hoping you'd buzz me in." The message causes her to swiftly look out of the window. She spots Royal's all black Cadillac truck parked next to her Jeep Cherokee. She looks taken aback by his assertiveness. She decides his actions warrant a call instead of a text.

"Hello?" He answers on the first ring.

"Royal, what are you doing here? Especially when I didn't invite you over?"

"I was just driving around aimlessly and I thought it would be romantic if I came to see you."

"No, that's not romantic! That's creepy!" Cleo shouts louder than she means to do. Royal gets embarrassingly quiet, making her feel bad.

"Understood," he says sternly. She takes a deep breath.

"But since you drove all of this way, I guess I could let you in-"

"Don't do me any favors," Royal spits out nastily. He uses the same voice he did when they first encountered each other and she cringes up at the negative memory.

"Royal, I didn't mean to yell, and I'm sorry if-"

"I'll see you at work tomorrow, Ms. Strong." He hangs up before she's able to get another word in. She tosses her cellphone to the couch with a look of regret covering her face.

What have I done?"

***

"I have all of your documents prepped and ready to go," Cleo says as soon as Royal walks inside of their office. He doesn't even look in her direction.

"Thank you, Ms. Strong." She watches him disappear behind the divider. She gets up from her desk to follow him.

"I also took the liberty of checking the productivity numbers from last week. 98% — not bad."

"Who's responsible for the lacking 2%? I want them in my office by the end of the day."

"But Royal, 98% is awesome! It's damn near perfect-"

"But it's not perfect, is it?" He exclaims, finally looking at her. It almost seems like he's talking about them and not the job. She makes a startled expression.

"No, it's not, but-"

"But nothing! This is the reason why I'm the management professional and you're my assistant. You assist me! You don't think, and you damn sure don't make any decisions."

She takes a step back from his aggressive demeanor, "Understood, sir. I'll get on it right away." She puts her back to Royal and moves towards her desk. She sits down angrily, *"Fuck! I've created a monster."*

***

Cleo looks around uncomfortably at all the occupants in the lunchroom. She chooses to sit as far away as possible from the other cackling employees scarfing down whatever they're eating for lunch today. She spots Pedra at her usual table but decides to walk past her. She finds an uninhabited space a few feet from where Pedra is sitting.

Cleo gives an unenthused glare to the salad on her tray. The truth is, she's not hungry, she was simply dying to get out of the uncomfortable office she shares with Royal. Things were so awkward between them that they barely said two words to each other. As soon as noon hit, she ran out of there. Unfortunately, she was so stuck on the issue she was having with Royal that she completely forgot about her issue with Pedra. She literally went from one uncomfortable situation to another: *Out of the frying pan and into the fire.*

"Hey, is this seat taken?" Pedra asks after approaching Cleo's table with her food tray. Cleo shakes her head.

"No, not at all." Pedra eases into the seat across from Cleo. Cleo tries not to engage with her.

"Not hungry?" Pedra asks, trying to make small talk with her old friend. Cleo sighs while pushing her tray away.

"Not really."

"Well, why not?" Cleo glances at Pedra but doesn't answer the question. Pedra lets out the deep breath she's been holding.

"Look Cleo, I said some things I shouldn't have said and I'm sorry."

"Thanks for apologizing, but that doesn't change what happened. You're my best friend, Pedra. I can't believe you really feel those ways about me." Both ladies tense up once the conversation officially becomes too serious for work.

"Look, I didn't come over here to rehash the hurtful past, I just wanted to let you know that I'm sorry." Pedra stands up and grabs her tray, "And when you're ready to talk, you know how to find me. See you later."

CHAPTER SIXTEEN

Cleo is used to being alone, but for some reason, the loneliness she feels tonight is different. Her apartment walls seem to be closing in on her. She has this dark cloud hovering over her head that she can't shake. She has no one to talk to… no one to be there for her while she's feeling like she's feeling now. Her phone hasn't made a sound in so long that she had to make sure it was still on. Now, she's pacing the floor like a mad woman. She's so antsy that she can't sit still. She has to get out of here tonight, but where should she go?

"Fuck it. I'm going to the bar."

Cleo throws on an outfit she hasn't worn in forever. It shows too much boob and far too much leg, but she's craving attention so badly that it doesn't matter how she gets it. She applies a nice amount of "hoe-red" colored lipstick to her full lips and stares at herself in the mirror.

"Ok, here goes nothing," she mumbles before heading out to experience a nightlife she hasn't purposely sought out since she was in college. Even back then, she had a partying buddy. Now that she's solo, she needs to be more cautious. She still plans on having a good fucking time, though. *"Fuck people. I don't need a partner to turn up tonight."*

Cleo realizes quickly that she has no idea where to go. Since she doesn't hang out much, she's ignorant when it comes to clubbing spots. Before she allows her inexperience to irritate her, she decides to head back to the place where Pedra took her on the night she met Donte.

"Well, I wanted to do something, so that hole in the wall is better than nothing."

Even though it's only been a week since she last visited the bar, the atmosphere seems totally different. When she was there last, the crowd was a bunch of middle-aged folks going through their own versions of midlife crises. The people there tonight are nearly the polar opposite. It's a sea of 20-something year olds that seem to be living their best lives. Cleo is trying her best not to feel out of place, but she can't help but to feel that way.

As soon as she walks in, her eyes go straight to the table from the infamous blind date night. A group of young women are sitting there now. They are laughing nonstop at whatever it is they're going on and on about. They seem to be having a great time. Cleo smiles at the sight as if she can remember those days.

She slides through the crowd to get to the busy bar. She spots the unpleasant bartender from last time and throws her hand up to get her attention. She speeds over to her.

"What'll it be?" She spits out hurriedly.

"Long Island, top shelf," Cleo shouts over the loud music. The lady scurries off before Cleo's able to hand over her form of payment. She sets her debit card on the bar in front of her.

"Excuse me, miss. Do you mind if I join you?" Cleo turns around to face the man's voice coming from behind her. She makes a fucked-up expression at the sight of Donte.

"Ugh, don't talk to me!" She exclaims in the most unpleasant voice she can conjure up. She tries to put her back to him, but he stops her.

"Cleopatra, please, just let me apologize-"

"Fuck that! Absolutely not! I gave you a second chance for a first impression and you blew it! You're an awful person, Donte, and I never want to talk to you again!"

"Cleo, please," he pleads again. She successfully turns away from him to wait for her drink. He steps as close as he can to the back of her without his body pressing against hers. He begins whispering in her ear, "You're right, I'm awful. I'm a fucking douchebag. Ever since I said those terrible things to you, I've been nothing but embarrassed. My mother didn't raise me that way, and she'd roll over in her grave if she knew I talked to a woman like that. Cleo, I can't express how sorry I am. That was fucked up of me. I would love to ask you for another chance, but I know you're going to say no."

"You're so right about that!" Cleo spits out without bothering to turn around to face him. She hands the bartender her card and tells her to start her tab, "So leave me the hell alone, Donte. Best of luck to you, and good riddance."

***

Cleo is feeling good. The music is right, the atmosphere is live, and that third Long Island she just swallowed down definitely hit the spot. *"Fuck my two-drink maximum. I'm doing what I want to do tonight."*

Cleo feels like dancing, even though it's been a very long time since she confronted a dance floor. She turns around and stares at the congested space. She glares at the intimidating moves the younger people are doing and decides that's not her thing. She opts to dance in place instead.

She raises her hand to signal to the bartender to bring her another drink. Her hips move on their own to a song with a funky beat blaring over the huge speakers. Before she knows it, her ass is jiggling, too. The people standing next to her at the bar slide over to give her the needed room to do her thing.

Cleo pulls out a few old moves that were hot when she was a young tenderoni. Her small dress rises up her thick thighs constantly while she shakes her lower half. She clutches the bottom of the thin garment to stop her vagina from showing. She dances provocatively until a man comes up behind her and grabs her around her waist. He sticks his pelvis against her nearly exposed cheeks.

Not caring who it is, Cleo grinds her ass across his crotch. She does it so many times that his dick gets hard. Cleo can feel his stiffening member through his denim pants. The feel of it sliding across her vagina makes her hot.

"Damn, Cleo. You're working that motherfucka," Donte points out with a bite of his lip. Cleo stops dancing at the sound of his voice. She turns around to face him.

"Too bad for you. You could've seen just how well I worked it if you wasn't such a fucking scumbag!" She slurs before reaching for her fourth drink. Donte looks concerned.

"I thought you had a two-drink maximum?"

"Fuck that and fuck you!" She exclaims nastily. She places her straw between her lips and takes a big gulp of her drink.

"Cleo, I really think you should slow down. I can't let you drive like this."

"I don't need you to worry about me. Mind your own damn business, Donte."

CHAPTER SEVENTEEN

Donte watches from afar as Cleo downs drink number four, and then five. A guy sitting next to her notices how drunk she is and starts whispering in her ear. After a few moments, he has his hand on her thigh. Donte decides he's seen enough. He walks over to intervene.

"Cleo, come on. It's time to go." Cleo shoves him away from her.

"Donte, I told you to leave me the fuck alone! Don't you see I'm having a conversation?"

"Cleo, you're drunk, so I think it's time for you to go home. Now." The unknown fellow next to Cleo stands to his feet.

"Fool, didn't she tell you to leave her alone? I'm claiming her tonight." Donte smirks at the man before lifting his hand and signaling someone. Two guys approach from different parts of the bar. They stop once they reach Donte's side.

"I really think you should find someone else to claim tonight. She's not going home with you," Donte says in a calm, but intimidating tone. The man eases backwards with his hands raised.

"Aye man, I don't want no trouble. I just wanted to have a little fun tonight, that's all."

Donte and his boys watch as the man disappears into the crowd. He turns his attention back to Cleopatra, who has her face laying on the bar. He sighs. "Bo, help me get her to my car."

Bo helps Donte carry a nearly passed out Cleo to his old school Mustang. They situate her in the front seat. Donte digs in her purse and grabs her keys. He hands them to Bo.

"I think I saw a gray Jeep Cherokee outside of her crib when I dropped her off the other night. When you find it, jump in it and follow me. I'm about to take her home."

Donte gets in his car and waits for Bo to appear behind him. Once he emerges from the parking lot, Donte pulls off. He glances over at a sleeping Cleo every few minutes. He does so until he pulls up outside of her apartment complex.

"Her space is right there," Donte informs Bo after he parks in a random spot and jumps out of his car. Bo parks Cleo's truck in her designated space as Donte eases her out of his car.

"Get the door," he commands Bo. Bo tries a few keys on her key ring before he gets to the one that opens the main door. They walk in and head down the hallway.

"Right here. Apartment 1103," Donte states. Bo tries out key after key again. He finally finds the right one and unlocks the door. Donte lays Cleo on the couch while Bo sets her keys on her table. Donte tosses Bo his keys.

"You can wait in the car. I'm going to make sure she's good before I go." Bo walks out of the door without responding to Donte's words. He closes the door behind him.

Donte looks down at a passed-out Cleo. He wants to help her to bed but deems that action a little too personal. He got her home safe and sound, which is good enough in his book. He leans down to kiss her on the forehead. He spots a notepad on her table. He decides to leave a note:

"Goodnight, Cleopatra. I owed you one. I'm not as bad as you think I am. A million times, I'm sorry.

-Donte"

***

Cleo has a headache that won't quit, and huge bags underneath her eyes to match.

"Thank God it's the weekend," she mumbles after peeling herself off the couch to make a fresh pot of coffee. She attempts to hydrate while waiting for its brewing to finish. She carries the glass of water to the table to stare at Donte's note for the tenth time.

She reads the words over and over again as if they're going to change on the page. She grins at the thought of Donte coming to her rescue and saving her from herself. Things could've ended very differently for her last night if he wouldn't have been there. She shutters at the possibilities.

Cleo is pouring her a hot cup of Joe when her text alert noise goes off. She unhurriedly checks it.

"Ms. Strong, where are you??? You should've been at the office an hour ago!" Confusion covers her face after she reads the text from Royal. She calls his phone.

"I hope you're calling me to inform me that you're on your way," Royal says as soon as he answers.

"On my way? What are you talking about?"

"What do you mean, 'what am I talking about'? Did you read your contract?" Cleo makes a weird face.

"I glanced over it," she admits. Royal sighs as if he's annoyed.

"Well, if you would've read it instead of glanced at it, you would've known that we work the third Saturday of every month. We have to comb through all the paperwork to make sure we're on track before the end-of-the-month deadlines." Cleo's mouth hangs open, but nothing comes out of it. Royal grows impatient, "Hello?"

"Yes, I'm here," she mutters.

"And that's the problem. Don't be there, be here. You have 20 minutes." Royal hangs up before she gets the chance to protest.

"Shit! What am I going to do?"

***

Cleo drags her body off the elevator and past the empty secretary's desk. She fixes the sunglasses on her face before opening Royal's office door. He's standing at his desk as if he's waiting for her.

"You're late."

"Thanks. We established that already," she expresses in a smart-aleck tone. She walks sluggishly towards her desk, but he stops her.

"Umm, where are you going? We have work to do." Cleo faces him with an evil glare.

"Look, Royal. Spare me, OK. I had a long night." Royal makes a face as if he's bothered by her statement. He tries to swallow down his growing jealousy.

"Well, sorry, Ms. Strong, but that has nothing to do with me. It wasn't like I was the one with you last night." She rolls her eyes while placing her hand on her hip.

"I don't know what you're trying to get at but let me tell you this: We're the only ones in this office today so I won't hesitate to cuss your ass out if you think you're going to talk to me like you talk to your other employees. You want us to work? OK, but don't for one second think I'm going to take your bullshit. Not today, Royal."

CHAPTER EIGHTEEN

"Well, everything seems to be in order, so we're all set for the start of May." Cleo takes a relieved breath after Royal's words. He sits back in his chair next to her while staring at the side of her face. He doesn't want to seem like he cares, even though he does more than he's willing to admit. His mouth starts moving without his brain's permission. It's an awful idea to pry, but he does so anyway.

"So, some time you had last night, huh?" He tries to ask lightly, referring to her clearly hung-over state. She starts separating paperwork into different stacks before acknowledging his inquiry.

"Yeah. It was crazy," she replies, opting to stay away from the juicy details. Royal tightens his jaw.

"Oh really? Crazy? Wow, that's an interesting way of putting it." He lets out a fake chuckle. Cleo cuts her eyes at him.

"If you have something you want to say, Royal, then just say it." He loosens his tie before suddenly sitting upright in his chair. He turns Cleo's body towards his body and pins her legs between his. His hands hold on to her chair arms tightly. He boxes her in while getting in her face.

"Did you fuck him?" He forces out angrily. Cleo laughs at the question, making his anger grow.

"Did I fuck who?"

"Whoever the fuck you were on a date with yesterday!"

"Royal, you need to chill. I wasn't on a date with anyone."

"Bullshit! I can smell his cologne all over you!" He shouts louder, startling Cleo. His words make her remember that she failed to shower after she got in last night because she was too fucked up; And this morning, Royal rushed her out the house so fast that she barely got a chance to brush her teeth. Did she smell like Donte? Probably, but he and she were *definitely not* on a date. That, she's not lying about. All of the other details are none of Royal's business.

"No, you're the one that's full of shit, Royal! You retreated from me the moment I said something you didn't like instead of talking it out like a fucking adult! Then, you started calling me Ms. Strong like our relationship was strictly professional again, and now you're sitting here acting like a jealous ass boyfriend! Get your shit together!"

The more she talks, the more furious she gets. She leans towards him, putting their faces within inches of each other, "What reason would I have to lie to you? It's not like you and I are dating or some shit! It's not like I'm fucking you!"

She yells her last statement near the top of her lungs. They stare at each other in an intimidating way, breathing hard from the intensity of the moment. Their body language suggests that a fight is about to ensue but their eyes say they're more interested in a *different* form of physical combat. For some reason, they're totally turned on right now, and they both know it. The temperature has skyrocketed in the room. Royal licks his lips.

"I told you, you're mine."

"Sorry, Royal, but at this very second, I don't belong to anyone."

Royal's nostrils flare like a wild bull. He takes her words as a form of disrespect, even though he's not sure why. He uses his adrenaline as the fuel he needs to finally kiss Cleo. Even though she's been waiting for this moment for a long time, the passionate gesture still surprises her.

The power behind their first smooch is something they've never felt before. Sparks fly when Royal wraps his manly arms around Cleo and sticks his warm tongue down her throat. Cleo's shock is quickly replaced with an enormous feeling of ecstasy. She challenges his tongue with hers, causing Royal's blood to boil over with sexual desire.

"I have to have you," Royal confesses after suddenly jumping up from his chair. He slides all of his desk's contents to the floor before snatching Cleo to her feet. He picks her up with ease and lowers her on top of the stable wood furniture. He spreads her legs wide to get in between them.

"You don't belong to me, huh?" He snarls while ripping a hole in the crotch of her stockings. His lips find hers again as he moves the seat of her panties to the side to caress her clit.

"Mm…" Cleo moans when he finds her pleasure button. His fingers sweep across her hardening clitoris using the perfect rhythm. He unfastens his pants and lets them fall to his ankles. His rock-hard dick makes an appearance through his boxer's fly.

"You may deny that you belong to me, but your pussy knows it's mine," he spits out, sliding Cleo's round bottom towards his pelvis. He tears her panties to shreds, exposing her wet pussy underneath. His dickhead finds her entrance effortlessly. He slides inside of her without giving it a second thought.

"Shit, Royal! Wait!" Cleo cries out. Requesting the use of a condom briefly crosses her mind, but the feel of his huge, raw dick inside of her sends that thought out of the window. Royal responds to her concerns by sticking his tongue between her lips. He gets in the ideal stance to stroke her slowly. The more he explores the depths of her, the juicier her cave becomes. Royal moans once her interior walls officially embrace him.

"Damn, baby. That's right. Let me in." The talent behind Royal's hip thrusts are breathtaking. Cleo's legs shiver once he prods at her G-spot. He notices her reaction and pokes at it again.

"Shit, Royal! That's my fucking spot!"

"I know. I can feel it," he boasts. He hits it again, and again, and again. He does so repeatedly until she shivers with an orgasm.

"Ohh shit, Royal! Oh Shit!" She expresses with tightly closed eyes. She lays her back against his desk while continuing to take a pounding from a man that knows how to work his endowments. He takes the opportunity to place her thick legs on his shoulders. He grabs her waist and guides himself to her spot again. She shivers with a second orgasm.

"Ohh! Ohh shit!" She chants again. His stroke game is nothing short of extraordinary. Cleo wants to tap out, but she refuses to let Royal think he's conquering her…
Even though he is.
"I want to cum so bad, but this shit feels so fucking good," he admits without fucking up his rhythm. Cleo can barely hear him due to another orgasm she's experiencing. "I can fuck you like this all day, you know that? I can fuck you on my desk until the cleaning crew gets here tonight."

"No!" Cleo whines, deciding that she can't cum anymore without losing consciousness. It's been a long time since she had sex, so Royal's skillful ass is overloading her body.

"Oh, so you want me to wrap it up, huh?" Royal asks cockily. He fucks with her spot again, causing her legs to shake violently.

"Yes! Please!" She's able to get out before cumming again. Royal smirks.

"If you want me to cum, all you have to do is tell me it's mine."

"It's yours!" Cleo shouts with no hesitation. Her relinquishing possession of her pussy to Royal does something to him. He bangs her harder. "Shit, Royal! I said it's yours!" She shouts before another orgasm takes her breath away. Her body stiffens up from the constant spasming.

"What's mine?" Royal asks through broken breaths. He brushes the sweat dripping from his brow.

"This pussy!" She shrieks.

He bites down on his lip while stroking her harder, "What else is mine?"

"I'm yours!"

Cleo can tell by the look on his face that he's nearing his peak. He grunts, "You're mine, huh?"

"Yes, I'm yours!"

"You're my girl?"

"Yes, I'm your girl!"

"Fuck!" Royal screams, snatching his throbbing cock from Cleo's swelling vagina. He jacks it until he shoots sperm on her inner thigh. He places his hand on his desk to stop himself from falling. Exhausted, they look at each other.

"Wow, that was amazing," Cleo compliments, sitting up on her elbows.

"Tell me about it," he breathes out while trying to catch his breath. He locks eyes with her, "And I've been told you you're my woman. Now, I'm just glad you're finally seeing things my way."

CHAPTER NINETEEN

Royal's bed is a lot more comfortable than Cleo ever imagined it would be. The luxurious mattress and expensive sheets hug her back while Royal's chocolate ass devours her front. He makes love to her body with slow, accurate thrusts. She moans into his mouth while he kisses her deeply.

"Shit, I'm going to cum," Royal whispers before stroking her a few more times. He guides his dick out of her, allowing his ejaculate to squirt all over her stomach. Cleo cringes up at the feel of it.

"Royal— again? I just got out of the shower," she mentions in an annoyed voice. He rolls off of her and lands on his back.

"Shit, my bad, baby. I needed somewhere to cum, unless I cum inside-"

"A condom," Cleo finishes his statement. He looks over at her.

"No. I was going to say inside of you." Cleo gawks at him like he's insane. She jumps up from his bed and rushes to the restroom before Royal's DNA drips anywhere. He enters the bathroom just in time to watch her turn the shower on. She steps inside of it immediately. He decides to join her in the huge cleansing space.

"I see you know how to work the shower now," he points out amusingly. She cuts her eyes at him.

"Of course I do. This is my third one in four hours. Ever since you had me spread eagle on your desk earlier today, we've been fucking nonstop. You won't let me stay clean."

"Do you really want me to," he asks, taking a dominant step in her direction. He hangs over her like a domineering tree. She stares into his eyes.

"Um," she mumbles, allowing his sexy presence to mentally distract her. He leans down and kisses her lips.

"See, you want me inside of you right now. I can see it in your eyes."

"At least we'll be in the shower this time. That way, you can cum near the drain and not on me."

"You mean *in you*?" Royal says again. Cleo breaks their eye contact.

"Royal…" she mutters, turning to grab her washcloth from its hanging position. He spins her around to regain her attention.

"What? Why won't you address that? Every time I mention it, you try to avoid the conversation."

"Because, you're just joking. You can't possibly mean that." He stares at her with a dead serious look, making her eat her words. "Royal, how can you be serious about not pulling out? We just started sleeping with each other today. I haven't had time to go and see my doctor, get on birth control-"

"Who said anything about birth control?"

"Ha!" She spits out obnoxiously before turning her back to him again. She chuckles at his shocking rebuttal while rinsing her body. "I know you're joking now. Why would you want to cum in me without birth control unless you are trying to get me pregnant?" She feels his body suddenly press against her backside. He wraps his arms around her waist.

"Maybe because I am." She freezes up after his words.

"Royal, you're just talking shit right now because that's crazy," she points out in a disbelieving tone.

"I agree, it is crazy, but I'm 100% serious. I want a baby, and you'd make a great mom. We're not spring chickens anymore, Cleo. We're running out of time to start a family." She turns towards him, revealing the perplexed expression covering her face.

"There's so much wrong with your statements that I don't know where to begin." Royal looks offended, but Cleo keeps talking, "First of all, you started off your point by saying 'you' want a baby, not 'we'. The truth is, you have no idea what I want because we've never talked about that. We've honestly never talked about anything that deals with a relationship because ours just started today! What about love? What about marriage? What about vowing to be together forever? Aren't those things important enough to establish first before deciding to start a family together?"

She pauses for a response, but he doesn't provide one. She continues, "Second of all, you're right, we're not spring chickens anymore, so why would I jump at the idea of getting pregnant with all of the complications that come along with having a baby at my age? Did I want to have a baby once upon a time? Sure, but having one now? I'm not so sure about that."

***

"Really, Royal? How long are you going to ignore me?" Cleo asks the back of his head. She's preparing dinner while he's sitting on the couch facing the TV. He answers her without turning around.

"I already told you, Cleo, I'm not ignoring you."

"The hell you aren't! Ever since we talked about the baby thing, you barely said two words to me. Plus, how the hell are we having a cook-off if you won't come into the kitchen?"

"Because you're using the stove right now. I can wait until you're done." Cleo glances at the massive range with a sigh.

"That's bullshit, Royal! This stove is big enough for the both of us to cook on and you know it."

The room grows quiet while Cleo waits for a response. Royal expels a deep breath before standing to his feet. He joins her near the refrigerator.

"You're right, it is," he agrees. He finally looks at her for the first time since they exited the shower. She steps into his personal space.

"Babe, talk to me. If our relationship is going to work, then we have to be able to confide in one another." He hesitates to address her statement as if he's afraid of speaking his mind. He grabs her hand gently.

"I know the whole 'me getting you pregnant' thing sounds insane to you, but I can't help how I feel. When I was with my fiancé, I went into full family mode. I was expecting to be a husband and a father. I was really looking forward to it, so when she left, all of my dreams came crashing down. I didn't know I was still in that mode until you came along. Now that I'm with someone again, it's almost like my mind picked back up where it left off. I see you and I see my future, and even though this shit is hard as hell for me to say to you right now, I still want you to hear it. I know we've only known each other for a week, Cleo, but I would love to see how far things can go with us. I'm all in if you are. I hope that doesn't scare you."

CHAPTER TWENTY

"Cleo, got a minute?" Cleo turns around at the sound of Pedra's voice before opening her car door. Pedra stares at her awkwardly, "I've been trying to catch up with you at lunch, but I haven't seen you in the cafeteria all week."

Cleo watches a few of her co-workers pass by them in the job's parking structure. Her eyes go back to Pedra, "Yeah, I eat lunch with Royal now. We usually go out for our food." Pedra processes the information with a head nod.

"That's cool. It seems like you and him are really having a good time together." Cleo can't help but to smile at the thought of her man.

"You're right, we are." Pedra smiles back.

"I'm happy for you Cleo, seriously. I really mean it." Cleo is secretly relieved to hear those words come from her friend's mouth. Her smile widens.

"Thank you, Pedra. That means so much coming from you."

Both women stare at each other as if they want to fall into their old, homegirl routine, but their apprehension won't allow it. One thing's for sure, however; they missed each other terribly. Pedra clears her throat.

"I came over here because I really needed to tell you something."

"What? Is everything OK?" Cleo asks, taking a concerned step towards Pedra. Pedra nods her head yes quickly.

"Oh yeah, everything is fine. Actually, everything is better than fine." Pedra holds up her left hand with excited eyes, revealing the elegant diamond ring sitting on her ring finger. Shock floods Cleo's face.

"Oh my God, girl! Congratulations!" She shouts, causing the few people walking past them to stare in their direction. "Shit, Pedra! Your ring is gorgeous!"

Cleo nearly snatches off Pedra's arm to get a better look at it. She studies the sparkle radiating from the single, princess-cut diamond.

"Thank you! Connor proposed to me last weekend. I know him and I have only been together for a few months, but this just feels right, you know?"

Cleo nods her head as if she completely understands. She and Royal have only known each other for two weeks and they practically live together. *In fact, she's on her way to his house right now.*

"As long as you're happy, I'm all for it. So, when are you guys talking about jumping the broom?" Pedra makes a weird facial expression.

"Next month. We're planning on going to Vegas."

"Next month!" Cleo exclaims, drawing more attention to them, "That is very short notice!"

"I know, I know. Everyone is saying that. Him and I are really ready to do this, though. He actually wanted to do it next week, but I told him that was entirely too soon. I have to give my family and friends time to make travel arrangements, and you— I want you to be my Maid of Honor."

***

"...So tomorrow, we're supposed to go with her to help pick out her wedding gown and our dresses, and then after that, her, the bridesmaids, and I are going to grab a bite to eat. Then, on Sunday, they're having a get-together-"

"What about our plans? I thought we were going to spend the weekend together?" Royal questions in a bratty tone. Cleo smacks her lips at him.

"Babe, stop it. I've been with you every second of every day since we became official. If we're not at your place together, then we're at mine. Aren't you ready for a break from us yet?" Royal wraps his arms around Cleo's waist before kissing her deeply. His tongue makes circles around hers, causing Cleo to moan softly. Their lips separate.

"A break from us? You're talking nonsense, baby. We're just getting started." Cleo blushes.

"Mmhmm… you say that now. I hope you mean that in another five years."

"I'll mean that forever."

Royal stares in Cleo's eyes in a way that makes her nervous. She takes a step away from him, "What happened to your meeting with the CEO? I remember Tava giving you a message about Mr. Collins coming down to meet with you this week, but you haven't mentioned anything about it since." Cleo hurries to change the subject. Royal follows her to his couch.

"Oh, yeah. I meant to tell you: He sent me an email about rescheduling the meeting to a later date, but he didn't specify when. He's a very busy man, so I get it, but I just wish he'd give me a definite day so I can be prepared, you know?" Cleo shakes her head as if she agrees. They flop down on the sofa.

"Are you going with me to Pedra's wedding shower on Sunday?"

"Wedding shower? Don't you mean bridal shower?" Cleo shakes her head no.

"Nope, I mean a wedding shower. It's for her and Connor, like a coed thing." Royal looks unenthused.

"Cleo, I really don't feel comfortable with that. I don't do well with huge crowds, and besides, she's one of my employees. What would I look like popping up at her personal event?"

"Like my date," she answers quickly. "But, if you don't want to go, I won't make you. I'll go by myself-"

"And leave you out there dangling in front of all of those cock hounds? Absolutely not." He pecks Cleo on the lips before grabbing the bowl of popcorn from the table. He leans back on the couch and Cleo leans back on him. "There's no way I'm letting my lady step out solo. If you want me there, then I'm there."

***

Royal munches all over Cleo's clit as if he has a taste for her flavor. He doesn't give her head that often, but when he does, it's magical. Cleo's body jerks when he edges her clitoris with his tongue. He moans while he drinks her. Shallow breaths fill her chest.

"Shit, Royal! Oh my God! Don't stop!" She screeches. Her thighs' spasmic movements signal to him that she's nearing her climax. Royal locks on to her swollen pearl, rolling his wet tongue over it like a wave. She grabs his head and rides his tongue like a surfboard.

"Shit! Shit! Shit!" She sings in a high octave. Her back arches once her body releases its built-up tension inside of Royal's mouth. He courteously cleans up behind himself by sucking up all of her orgasm fluid. She shivers sporadically until he stops.

"Lay back and relax. I'm not done yet."

Royal gives Cleo some of the best dick she's ever had in her life. She announces her twelfth orgasm in 15 minutes. Royal watches the blissfulness covering her face while filling her up with his flawless cock. He glares at her sexily.

"Uh huh… I got you now, Cleopatra. I know exactly how to please your body."

Cleo is so high off of Royal's loving that she can barely hear his words. She forces her head to the side to let out another shriek of satisfaction.

"Fuckkk Daddyyy!" She yells loudly. Royal's room walls vibrate with the sounds of her pleasure. Royal wrestles with his own orgasm as long as he can.

"Baby, can I?" He asks through shallow breaths. Cleo doesn't hear him.

"Baby, I want to. Can I?" He inquires again, shivering with an impending orgasm. Cleo gawks at him.

"Can you what?" She asks after he finally gets her attention.

"I want to stay in it. Please tell me I can stay in it," he whispers with his kissable lips near her ear. He starts nibbling on her lobe, distracting her for a second.

"No, Royal. We're not ready for that."

"But I am," he says with a quiver, scaring the shit out of Cleo.

"But we're not," she reminds him. His body twitches, which Cleo knows is an intro to his last stroke. She pushes him off of her a split second before his penis erupts. He cums in her pubic hair instead of inside of her. Cleo jumps up angrily.

"Royal! What the fuck were you thinking?" She demands to know in a very unpleasant voice. He looks taken aback by her tone.

"Excuse me?"

"You heard me! That one little impulsive decision could've changed everything for us for the rest of our lives! I told you I'm not ready for that, but your ass never listens!"

"Hold up. I understand you're mad or whatever, but I deserve more respect than you're giving me right now."

Cleo flips him off before putting her back to him. He stands to his feet.

"Wow! You're really gonna double-down on the disrespectful shit, huh?" He walks around to the front of her, "So let me tell you this, then, I don't allow disrespectful people in my house."

She folds her arms across her bare chest while glaring at her naked lover, "Say less. I'll get my shit and go."

CHAPTER TWENTY-ONE

Cleo giggles with Pedra and her bridesmaids even though she feels like shit. Ever since her and Royal had their first argument last night, she hasn't been able to think about anything else since. She still can't believe things got that ugly between them, but he was tripping if he thought she was going to let him cum in her without her permission. She runs her body, not him…

So why does she feel like she made the wrong choice, then?

"Cleo? You good, girl?" Pedra asks while staring in her direction. The three ladies that make up the remainder of the wedding party look at her as well. A fake smile covers her face.

"I'm OK. I was just thinking about something."

"I can tell. I've asked you the same question like three times."

"Oh, I'm sorry, Pedra. What is it?"

"We've narrowed it down to these two dresses, but I'm having a hard time deciding between them. As of right now, the votes are tied, two to two. We need you to be the tie breaker."

Cleo stares at the two gowns Pedra is pointing at hanging on the rack behind her. She picks the simpler gown with the sweetheart neckline.

"I like that one more. It's subtle, but elegant." Pedra smiles with a head nod.

"See! That's why you're my Maid of Honor and not these bitches. You and I always see eye-to-eye!" The other ladies smack their lips at Pedra's facetious statement. Pedra ignores them and throws her hand up to get the bridal shop worker's attention.

"Excuse me— miss! I'll take this one!" She shouts instead of waiting until the petite lady makes it within ear range. She glances at the dress Pedra is referring to.

"Excellent choice, ma'am," she says in a tone that suggests she says that to all of the customers. She checks the size of the gown.

"This is the size you requested, which is a size six. We do free alterations if any part of the dress is too small or too big, so you're free to try it on now so we can take a look at it-"

"Excuse me, did you say a six?" Pedra cuts the lady off to ask. The worker shakes her head yes.

"Yeah. That's the size you requested when you called last week, right?" Pedra makes a weird face.
"No. Actually, I said a 10, not a six." The lady stares down at the paper in her hand.

"I'm sorry, ma'am, but I could've sworn you said a six. I took your call myself. That's what I have written down right here." She tries to show Pedra the paper, but Pedra refuses to look at it. The lady continues, "Sorry, that must've been my mistake. I'll get you your correct size right away."

She scoops up the dress and hurries to the back. Pedra looks embarrassed, but tries to play it off, "I swear, you can't find any good help nowadays." Her bridesmaids laugh, but Cleo doesn't find her words funny. She knows that Pedra wears a six, so why is she sizing up all of a sudden?

"She doesn't look like she's gaining weight," Cleo thinks to herself after looking her friend up and down, *"But her clothes are a bit baggier than she usually wears them. Something must be up."*

"Cleo, don't you agree? That was some bullshit, right?" Pedra throws out there, trying to get Cleo to cosign her apparent diversion. Cleo nods her head slightly.

"Yeah, you're right about that. It's definitely some bullshit going on."

***

Cleo watches Pedra closely as the ladies gossip over lunch. Everyone else at the table ordered glasses of wine, but Pedra never glanced at the alcohol menu. She also ordered something light to eat, which is totally unlike her. Pedra can easily eat two burgers and an order of fries without batting an eyelash. Now, she's barely touching her salad. Every time she takes a bite, she looks like she could vomit. Cleo gawks at her until she decides she's seen enough.

"Pedra, can you come to the ladies' room with me for a second?" She asks while standing up. Pedra agrees and follows her. They enter the empty bathroom a few moments later. Cleo turns to face her.

"Is that why you're marrying Connor? Because you're pregnant?" Cleo inquires, deciding to get straight to the point. Pedra looks shocked.

"Cleo! How do you know I'm pregnant? Oh my God, do I look fat?" She questions quickly, staring at herself in the huge mirror. She smooths her shirt over her bloated stomach a few times. Cleo disagrees.

"No, you don't look fat, but I know you, Pedra. You do wear a size six, and you definitely love wine, and a salad for lunch? Forget about it. Only as an appetizer-"

"Alright! I get your point," Pedra states as if Cleo's words are embarrassing her. She makes a worried face.

"My family would kill me if I had a baby without being married first. Having a child out of wedlock is a huge no, no in my household."

"Pedra, you're a grown ass woman. You don't have to live your life according to your family's values if they're not your own. Connor seems like a nice guy, but marriage? That's a huge commitment."

"So is having his baby." Cleo agrees with Pedra.

"You're right, but you're already pregnant. The damage is done. You're not already married, though, so you still have time to make the right decision for you. Don't jump into something you're not ready for."

Pedra is not sure what to say, so she remains silent. Cleo puts her hand on her friend's shoulder, "If you need me, I'm here, and if you really want to marry Connor, then I'll be right by your side being the best Maid of Honor I can possibly be; but until then, congratulations on the baby. You're going to be a great mother."

CHAPTER TWENTY-TWO

Cleo rummages through her purse for the third time as she and the ladies walk out of the restaurant door. She was so embarrassed when her bill came for her food and she couldn't pay it because she didn't have any money on her. Pedra paid for her lunch and Cleo promised to pay her back as soon as she got the funds. Somehow, she managed to misplace her debit card and she has no idea where it could be. She was going to cancel it until she checked the bank's online app and noticed it hadn't been used recently. Since her solo night out last week, no new transactions have been made.

"You just misplaced it, Cleopatra. You have a lot on your mind," she tells herself while looking up at the warm, springtime sun. She sighs out loud.

After she stormed out of Royal's house nearly 18 hours ago, she hasn't heard a peep from him. She typed him a dozen text messages but erased every last one of them before she could hit send. She misses him, but she doesn't want to be the first person to reach out. *She's not sure how long she can keep up this charade, though.*

"Connor! Hi!" Pedra says happily, causing Cleo to tune back into reality. She looks in their direction just in time to see Pedra greet her soon-to-be-husband with a kiss. Cleo pauses in her tracks once her eyes land on Donte. He grins in her direction.

"What are you fellas doing here?" Pedra asks after they separate.

"We just wrapped up at the tuxedo place, so I decided to come down here to get a bite to eat with you. I see we're too late, though."

Pedra nods her head before falling into a personal conversation with him. Donte greets the other ladies, causing each one of them to blush uncontrollably. He ignores their smitten glares while moving in the direction of Cleo.

"Good afternoon, Cleopatra," he says with a smile. She can't help but to smile back.

"Good afternoon, Donte." He glances around at the nosy women surrounding them.

"You got a minute?"

"Sure," she responds, turning around and walking towards the restaurant's parking lot. She pulls her cell phone and keys from her purse. They move about slowly.

"I just wanted to apologize again for the way I acted on our first date-"

"There's no need for that, especially after you got me and my truck home safely the other night. If anything, I should be apologizing to you for the inconvenience."

"It was no problem. It was the least I could do for disrespecting you the way I did. That wasn't cool at all." Cleo nods her head that she agrees but doesn't vocalize it. Things slowly become awkward between the two of them.

"I'm not going to lie, I was looking forward to hearing from you after that night, but you never reached out."

"Actually, it crossed my mind. I wanted to thank you personally, but we never exchanged numbers, remember?" Cleo reminds Donte.

"Oh, yeah. That's right. Well, we seriously need to rectify that." Donte grabs Cleo's phone from her hand and dials his number. His phone starts ringing a moment later. He hangs up, "Make sure you lock me in; and Cleo, I really hope you're coming to the party tomorrow. I would really love to see you there."

***

Cleo stares at her cluttered bed and sighs. She has pulled out nearly every garment she owns, and she still hasn't been able to find the perfect outfit to wear to Pedra and Connor's wedding shower tomorrow. She would love to have this conversation with Royal right now, but they still haven't broken their stubborn code of silence. He's surprisingly great at putting fashion together, and since he was going to be her date, she would've wanted to wear the same color he was wearing. Now that they're beefed out, she has to step out dateless tomorrow night. She's kind of glad, though. *After all, Donte is going to be there, and she's kind of looking forward to chatting with him again.*

She stares at the pile of clothes until her eyes hurt. She decides she needs a break. She heads to the kitchen to search her fridge for dinner options. She reaches for the Romaine lettuce. *"Salad it is."*
"KNOCK! KNOCK! KNOCK!"

Cleo nearly drops her food at the sound of someone beating at her door. She closes her refrigerator and cautiously heads towards it.

"Who is it?" She shouts before her eye peers through the peephole. She spots her handsome boyfriend and gasps out loud, "Royal? How did you get through the main entrance?" She swings her door open at the end of her inquiry. He extends the flowers in his hand towards her before answering.

"I waited until someone walked out of it. I've been in the parking lot for nearly an hour." She steps to the side with a confused look on her face. She grabs the beautiful, red roses on his way past her.

"Well, why didn't you call me? I would have buzzed you in." He takes off his blue jean jacket and lays it across the chair sitting next to Cleo's couch. He turns to face her.

"I know. Honestly, I wasn't sure if I wanted to come in or not. I'm pissed at you, and when I'm pissed at someone, I can ignore their existence until the end of time, but it's just something about you…" he moves closer to her, "...That I need. I miss you, Cleo."

He gazes at her like she's his dream come true. She swallows the growing lump of nervousness in her throat, "I miss you, too."

He wraps his manly arms around her waist before going straight for her lips. He kisses her with so much passion that she swears the lights in her apartment are flickering. They separate after their bodies heat up. She wipes the moisture from her mouth.

"But I'm pissed at you, too, Royal. We need to talk about boundaries and what's OK and not OK; and I need to know that you're going to respect them." He gestures that he agrees.

"I can do that, as long as we talk about my boundaries as well. You disrespected me, Cleo, and that can never happen again. One more incident like that, and I'm out the door. I'm serious."

CHAPTER TWENTY-THREE

Royal helps his girlfriend pick out the perfect shirt and skirt for Pedra's event tomorrow. She glances at him in awe, "I swear, babe, I've been looking at my clothes for over an hour and I never saw that combination." She lays the sexy, black pencil skirt on the back of her vanity chair and places the black, lacy blouse on top of it.

Royal holds her from behind, "There's something so sexy about a woman in all black. You're going to look stunning tomorrow by my side. I can't wait to show you off."

Cleo feels uneasy at the thought of Donte seeing her with Royal, even though she's not completely sure why. It's not like she likes Donte— *does she?*

"I feel the same way about you," she says, trying her best to get Donte off of her mind. She spins around to face her guy, "I'm sure you're going to look great in whatever it is you're wearing, too."

"Yeah, I'll be pretty fair for a square. I'm wearing all black as well." Cleo smiles at the news.

"Aww, so you want us to match, huh? I was thinking the same thing, but I thought you'd think that was a silly idea." Royal smiles, too.

"There's nothing wrong with matching your lady, as long as she's not wearing lime green or something crazy like that." Cleo laughs.

"I agree with you."

Royal helps Cleo clear off her bed while they laugh and talk about everything under the sun. Afterwards, they turn off the lights and he lays her body right where her pile of clothes used to be. He takes his time to cater to her sexual needs. Even though he's sore with her, he still wants her to know how sorry he is for his part in their problems.

Cleo shivers underneath Royal while he grinds his dick inside of her. She grabs his ass to force his hard cock deeper in her love canal. Her clenching vaginal muscles hug his penis just right. His chest vibrates overwhelmingly.

"If you don't want me to cum in you, I suggest you let me go," he warns her in a shaky voice. She releases him just in time for him to successfully pull out of her before he orgasms. She watches the blissfulness on his face once his ejaculate squirts on her leg.

"Fuck! I wish I could still be stroking you while I cum. I'd probably pass out."

"You and I both, but for different reasons," Cleo agrees in a joking tone. Royal climbs off of her. He slowly stands to his feet.

"Shit, baby. I'm dehydrated. I need some water. You need anything from the kitchen?"

"Nope, I'm good," Cleo replies, standing to her feet as well. She moves toward her master bathroom, "I need to clean you off of me, and when I get back, it's my turn to take advantage of your body."

Royal cheeses at the thought of her straddling him for a change. He watches her naked ass sashay into the restroom and close the door. He walks in the kitchen to get himself something to drink. He fetches him a glass of water and carries it to the couch. He sets it down before planting himself on the sofa. He looks around casually, "Damn. My girl is so dope."

He's thoroughly amazed by her cultured style. He hasn't met that many people in his lifetime that have embraced their African roots like Cleo has. That's definitely a trait he wouldn't mind his kids possessing. That's definitely a trait that more African Americans need to possess in this country.

His eyes go from her decor to his water. He picks it up quickly after realizing he set the glass down on her notepad. He curses himself when he spots the wet circle soaking through the pages. He flips it over to expose its dry side but pauses after he spots words that aren't in Cleo's handwriting. He reads them to himself, concluding with the signature at the bottom, *"Donte"*. Confusion floods his face. *"Who the fuck is Donte?"*

He carries the notepad to the room and sets it on the nightstand. He lays his nude body in the center of her bed. Cleo emerges from the bathroom a few moments later. She climbs on top of him without bothering to dry off.

"I hope you're ready for round two," she moans sexily before kissing on his neck. He doesn't respond to her advances. She halts as if she's offended.

"What's wrong?" She asks while staring in his eyes. He glares at her blankly, making her feel slightly uneasy.

"Who's Donte?" Her face reacts to the question before she can. He spots the apprehension in her eyes, causing his anger to bloom. He lifts her off of him, "You know what? I'm done with this shit. I should've followed my first mind and stayed the fuck away from you."

He smacks the notepad in her direction, causing it to land on the bed directly in front of her. She glances down at the note from Donte through distraught vision. Royal's words burn Cleo like a cattle prod to the heart. Tears gather in her eyes as she watches him get dressed.

"Donte is a guy I went on one date with before I met you, Royal. He has nothing to do with you and I."

"So you bring guys home on the first night, then? I had no fucking idea you were so promiscuous, Cleopatra. I guess I really should have put on that condom like you suggested, huh?" Cleo's mouth falls open after his harsh accusations. She stands to her feet angrily.

"First of all, I cannot believe you just said that to me! I can't even begin to tell you how disrespectful you are being! So, you think I'm a hoe now? Wow! You have some fucking nerve! Second of all, you need to stop drawing conclusions about scenarios you've made up in that delusional fucking head of yours! Yes, he and I dated. Yes, he brought me home, and no, I absolutely did not fuck him! You're out of line completely, Royal, and I want you to leave."

"My pleasure," he mumbles, sliding on his gym shoes. She tosses her robe on before following him to the door. She's tying its string when he turns around to face her.

"Maybe you're right, maybe we did rush into this," Royal spits out. He tries to appear unscathed, but the truth is, he's hurting himself by hurting her. Cleo brushes the tears away that are streaming down her face, making Royal feel like the asshole of the century. He tries to take a step towards her, but she forcefully places her hand on his chest.

"I was right, I can see that now. I just wish I would've listened to myself instead of believing in you."

CHAPTER TWENTY-FOUR

Even though Cleo's heart is shattered in a thousand pieces, she still finds the energy to drag herself to Connor and Pedra's wedding shower. She walks inside of the beautiful hall looking drop dead gorgeous, even though her mood couldn't be any uglier. Her feet carry her to the open bar immediately. She doesn't even bother looking for Pedra or Connor to congratulate them.

"Long Island, please," she says to the person overseeing the drinks. She stands at the stool-less area and waits for the young man to make her cocktail. She stares at the decorations all over the place that celebrate black love and tries not to vomit.

"Fuck love. Love ain't never been good to me."

"You made it," Donte says from behind her, pointing out the obvious. Cleo paints her face with a fake smile at the sound of his voice. She turns to look at him, nearly choking at the sight of his amazing appearance. His well-tailored suit fits his masculine body like a glove. She had no idea he could clean up so nicely.

"And we're matching. Wow, what are the odds?" He points out, referring to their all-black attire. She glances down at the outfit Royal picked out for her and sighs to herself.

"I don't know. I guess great minds think alike."

"Yeah, I think you're right."

Things get quiet between the two of them when their longtime friend, awkwardness, joins the conversation. They both face the bar.

"Let me guess? Long Island?" Donte asks when the bartender delivers her drink. Cleo grins.

"Yup. Long Island, my trusty go-to."

He chuckles, "Don't I know it. It's guaranteed to get you fucked up."

"Don't I know it," she repeats in a mocking tone. They both laugh.

"I know it's an open bar and all, but I'll be happy to leave a tip for you."

"No need. I'll take care of my woman's tip," Cleo hears from the other side of her, prompting her to rapidly turn in his direction. Her eyes grow wide at the sight of Royal. His jaw tightens with jealousy. Donte looks confused.

"Your woman?"

"Did I stutter?"

Royal takes a step towards Donte, but Cleo jumps in the middle of them. She places her hand on Royal's chest.

"Royal, please calm down. It's not what you think," she tries to convince him. Donte looks as if he disagrees but doesn't speak on it.

"It's not what I think? You have no idea what the fuck I think!" Royal blurts out loudly. He draws the attention of half of the party guests, which Cleo subsequently realizes are made up of his employees at Vella Industries. She gets embarrassed from the judging eyes.

"Look, man. I'm not trying to cause any problems. I was just kicking it with an old friend."

"Oh, really? An old friend? Well, I know all of my girl's friends and I've never heard of you before."

"Royal, you need to stop it! Now! Come on, we're leaving," Cleo says sternly. She grabs him by his hand to drag him away. Donte stops them.

"Oh yeah, Cleopatra, I forgot to tell you… I have your debit card. That night you got wasted and I took you home, you left it with the bartender. I told her I'd make sure to get it to you." He removes it from his wallet, "Here you go."

Cleo's face is mortified, but Donte looks amused. She snatches it from his hand quickly.

"Donte, is everything OK over here?" Connor inquires while emerging from the spectating crowd. Pedra appears right behind him.

"Donte?" Royal repeats with a perplexed look on his face. Donte smirks.

"Oh wait— don't tell me you have heard of me?" Royal's chest tightens up after Donte's facetiousness. Cleo grabs Royal's hand again.

"Royal, let's go."

"Yeah, Mr. Bradshaw. Maybe it is best you leave," Pedra spits out with a fold of her arms. He calms down after realizing he is making a big fool of himself.

"I'm so sorry Pedra and Connor," Cleo exclaims before dragging Royal towards the exit. She lets him go as soon as they reach the parking lot. The fire of a thousand hells are burning in her eyes when she decides to face him. He's looking at her the same way.

"You just embarrassed the shit out of me in there! Royal, what the fuck is wrong with you!"

"Wrong with me! What the fuck is wrong with you? We have one little problem and you ask another guy on a date the next day? Wow, does our relationship mean nothing to you?"

"Our relationship? What fucking relationship? Just last night, you told me that you should've followed your first mind and stayed away from me after calling me a hoe!"

"Well!" He points to the small building, "You and I had a falling out less than 24 hours ago and you're already dating another motherfucker!"

"Royal! I swear, I hate you so fucking much sometimes! Donte is not my date, he's Connor's brother! As in the Connor that's marrying Pedra!" A stupid look creeps across his face. Cleo continues, "He was going to be here whether I invited him or not! He's here for his brother, not for me!"

Cleo places her debit card in her purse and takes out her keys. She moves towards her truck, "You know what, Royal? This thing is getting too toxic for me. We seem to want two different things in life, we can't get along, and you just embarrassed me in front of half of the people at work! And Pedra— I owe her a huge apology for making a scene at a party that was supposed to be commemorating her special day. God, I feel so stupid-"

"Cleo, I love you," Royal blurts out, stopping her in her tracks suddenly. She wants to turn to face him, but she's too overwhelmed to do so. He takes steps in her direction, "Did you hear me? Baby, I said I love you."

Tears creep out of her eyes without her permission. She finally gives him eye contact, "No you don't, Royal."

"Yes I do. I love you, and I was afraid to tell you because I've never felt this way about anyone this quickly before. You have me so open that it's embarrassing. Look at what just happened! I'm running around here acting like an ass because you have me so far in my feelings that I can't control myself."

Cleo doesn't know what to say. Royal takes her silence as an invitation to get closer to her. He slides his arm around her waist.

"I know you feel the same way about me. I know you love me, too." She nods her head slightly, even though she's not 100% sure she's ready to admit it. He wipes the tears from her eyes.

"Tell me, then. I need to hear you say it."

"I'm scared," Cleo admits in a voice barely above a whisper. He lifts her chin until their eyes connect.

"I am, too, but I love you, Cleopatra, and I'll be damned if I waste one more second acting like I don't."

"I love you, too," she finally confesses. He smiles before laying a romantic kiss upon her lips. Things get hot and heavy between them without warning. *They have to have each other's bodies now.*

"Follow me to my place. I have something special to give you."

CHAPTER TWENTY-FIVE

By something special, Royal meant a good helping of make-up sex.

Royal eats Cleo from the back so well that she's not sure she can take it. He slurps all over her vagina and anus, causing her body to spasm out of control.

"Dammit, babe! You've never done anything this nasty before!" She expresses in amazement. He doesn't respond until she orgasms on his face. He finally comes up for air.

"I can put my mouth wherever I want on my woman. You officially have my heart, baby. Your body is my sexual playground."

His dick slides inside of her pussy walls before she's able to prepare for its girth. He guides it in as far as he can, shivering once her warmth surrounds his pulsating member. She wants to run, but he grabs her waist tightly. He rolls his hips behind her sensually, being careful not to hurt her. She relaxes enough to enjoy the penetration.

"Fuck, baby. I can barely handle the way you feel. I swear, I always want to climax after a few pumps," he admits in a low tone. His complimenting words motivate her to throw her ass back on him. Her participation catches him off guard.

"For real?" He asks with a bite of his lip. He pauses to let her skillfully twerk on his meat. The sight of her big ass bouncing turns him on. He smacks it sporadically until he nears an orgasm.

"Baby, let me cum in you," he mumbles. She continues to work her wet pussy on his swollen dick, trying not to get irritated by his repeated request.

"Royal, I can't," she responds without breaking her rhythm. His stomach vibrates with pleasure.

"We're going to be together forever as far as I'm concerned. I love you, Cleopatra, and I'm never going to let you go."

The sureness in his voice makes Cleo's heart skip a beat. His words put her in a trance. She bounces her moist ass against his pelvis harder.

"I'm telling you, baby, I'm about to explode! Please, don't stop!" He begs. He twitches with excitement.

She argues with herself internally, knowing she only has a few seconds to decide. She hesitates too long. Royal leans his body against hers and explodes deep within her. He growls loudly from the intense moment. She cringes up at the feel of his penis-head pumping sperm towards her cervix. He collapses on her back.

"Fuck! Shit!" He curses. Cleo lays flat on her stomach with Royal laying on top of her. He eventually rolls to the other side of the bed.

"There, are you happy now?" Cleo asks in an annoyed voice. He rolls her towards him and forces her to look into his eyes.

"There is nothing on this planet that has ever made me happier."

***

The sunlight hits Royal's face just right at the first sign of morning. Cleo has been up for a while, but she has yet to get out of bed. She's been staring at Royal's facial features, imagining what a baby with him would look like. She can't believe she let him cum in her last night. *What the hell was she thinking?*

She gets up to take a shower. She feels incredibly icky, and it doesn't help that a stream of bodily fluids run down her legs as soon as she stands up. She doesn't think she's ever been more repulsed in her life. She waddles straight to the bathroom.

Cleo is surprised to find Royal still asleep once she exits the restroom. She glances at the clock on his nightstand, noticing it's after seven in the morning. They have to be at work in 45 minutes. He needs to wake up.

"Royal," she exclaims, walking around to his side of the bed. His phone starts vibrating as soon as she makes it near him. She stares at the screen.

"Unknown?" she mumbles. The person hangs up, but then calls right back.

"Hello?" Cleo answers against her better judgment. The person on the other end doesn't say anything. Cleo speaks again.

"Hello?" Royal snatches the phone from her hand. He glances at the screen before hanging up. Cleo looks startled.

"What was that all about?"

"Why are you answering my phone?" He questions. She places her hand on her hip.

"Because, it rang— twice. And the better question is, why did you just snatch it away from me like that? Is there something you're trying to hide?"

Royal quickly denies her concern, "No, baby. Absolutely not. I get a lot of spam calls, that's all. I don't like answering them."

"Spam calls at seven in the morning?" Royal jumps up after noticing the time. He locks his phone and places it face down on the nightstand.

"I know, right. I said the same shit. I really have to find a way to block them." He kisses Cleo quickly before carrying his nude body towards the bathroom, "You should get dressed, baby. We don't want to be late for work."

***

Cleo works silently at her desk. She's been doing so since she and Royal arrived at the office. After walking into the building and glancing at eyes that witnessed Royal acting a hot fucking mess over her at Pedra's wedding shower, she's been in a self-conscious mood.

Royal keeps trying to act like he isn't fazed, but him being side-eyed from a few of his employees, including his secretary, has put him in a not-so-good mood, too. He walks to the edge of the divider to check on Cleopatra.

"Hey, baby. Is everything OK?" Cleo glances at him from her computer screen.

"Yes, Royal, everything is fine," she assures him, even though she's lying through her teeth. On top of her still being embarrassed by yesterday's shenanigans in front of her co-workers, those secretive phone calls Royal received this morning are making her feel uneasy. Something fishy is going on, she can feel it. She needs to get to the bottom of it before things become more complicated between her and her boss.

"It's almost lunch time. Where should we eat?"

"Actually, I thought I'd eat lunch in the cafeteria today. I really need to catch up with Pedra. Things got way out of hand at her wedding shower. I have to apologize for ruining her event."

CHAPTER TWENTY-SIX

The ugly looks Cleo is getting in the cafeteria seem to be worse than the stares she experienced this morning when she and Royal arrived at work. She tries to hide how uncomfortable she is, but the whispering that takes place after she passes each table has her ready to flee. She lets out a sigh of relief when she finally reaches her destination.

"Hey, Pedra. Do you mind if I join you?" Cleo asks with apprehension. Pedra sighs before looking up at her friend.

"It all depends… will Mr. Bradshaw be here to crash it?" Cleo rolls her eyes in her head at Pedra's sarcastic question. She eases down in the chair across from her.

"I get it, you're pissed at me, and I totally understand why."

"Pissed at you? Cleo, your unstable ass boyfriend ruined my wedding shower! He fucked up the whole atmosphere!"

"I know, I know, Pedra. That's why I'm here; I want to apologize. I had no idea he would act like that when he saw Donte. He fucking lost it-"

"How did Mr. Bradshaw know about Donte, anyway? Y'all went on one date. Don't tell me you told him about that?"

"Girl, hell naw! Actually, it's a long story…"
Cleo begins filling Pedra in, telling her about what happened on her solo night out. She told her how Donte

saved her, and she mentioned the note he left that she couldn't bring herself to throw away. Pedra smiles.

"So, that explains why he was acting the way he did when he saw you outside of the restaurant that afternoon. Mm, mm girl, Donte has a thing for you, and I ain't gonna lie, it seems like you have a thing for him, too."

Cleo hesitates to deny it. Pedra's eyes grow wide at the validation, "I knew it! I knew it! Girl, you better be careful with that. The last time Mr. Bradshaw suspected his lady was cheating, all hell broke loose."

"The last time?" Cleo perks up to ask. Pedra takes a sip of her water.

"Yup. The shit that happened with his wife. It was all the buzz around the office before I got here. Don't tell me you didn't hear about that?"

"Wife?!" Cleo chokes out. The elevation of her voice startles Pedra. Pedra glances around to make sure no one heard Cleo. She moves her seat closer to her stunned friend.

"Cleopatra, please do not tell me that you didn't know Mr. Bradshaw is married?"

"*Is* married?" Cleo forces out. Her head instantly starts to hurt. She's two seconds away from passing out. Pedra notices her distressed demeanor and grabs her arm.

"Cleo, let's take a walk. It looks like you need some air. Come on, girl. I got you."

***

Cleo's eyes are puffy and red by the time she and Pedra reach Pedra's car in the parking structure. They jump in before anyone can tell how distraught she is.

"Cleo, it's OK. Just take a deep breath," Pedra says in a soothing tone. Cleo nearly punches the dashboard at the thought of Royal lying to her.

"I'm going to kill him, Pedra. I'm going to fucking kill him!" She shouts loudly.

"I'm so sorry, Cleo. I thought you knew already. I know you've only been seeing him for a couple of weeks, but I thought he would've at least mentioned his wife. I mean, I knew they were separated, but I still thought he would've told you."

"He told me he was about to get married, not that he is married! Then, he said she cheated on him so he broke everything off." Pedra makes a face as if that's not what she heard. Cleo turns to face her.

"Pedra, you better tell me everything." Pedra sighs before facing her as well.

"OK, well, according to Tava, when she started working as his secretary, it was an analyst working in my spot named Lisa. She and Mr. Bradshaw eventually started dating, and after that, they jumped right into marriage. That's when Lisa said things changed between her and Mr. Bradshaw. She confided in Tava with a lot of their business, so Mr. Bradshaw fired her. He claimed he wanted a stay-at-home wife, but Tava knew Lisa was fired because she was exposing Mr. Bradshaw for the scum he truly was. Be that as it may, her and Tava still talked on the phone and she would tell her everything. Lisa said that Mr. Bradshaw was 'unbearable' as Tava put it, and that she needed to get away from him. Then, she found out she was pregnant and she nearly had a mental breakdown. She didn't want any ties to Mr. Bradshaw, so she went behind his back and got an abortion. When he confronted her about her weird behavior, she had to make up a lie so she told him she was seeing someone else. Tava said they got into it so badly that he hit her. That's when Lisa packed her shit and left his abusive ass."

Cleo stares straight ahead as if she can't believe what she's hearing. Pedra softly touches her hand, "Cleo, say something."

"Pedra, why didn't you tell me any of this before? You're supposed to be my best friend." Pedra takes a deep breath.

"I know, but when we got into it and I said those mean things to you, I told myself I wasn't going to say anything negative about your relationships again."

"But Pedra, this is stuff I needed to know!"

"Come on, Cleo. Think about it: If I would have told you this, you would've told me that I'm hating on you, or that I'm trying to sabotage your happiness or some shit. I decided to stay out of it."

"Yeah! And because you did, I ended up doing something so fucking stupid!" Cleo confesses, allowing new tears to run down her face. Pedra looks concerned.

"Do something stupid? What are you talking about?"

"Last night, I-" Cleo's throat burns. She swallows hard, "Last night, I let Royal cum in me." Pedra's eyes react to the news, but she refuses to comment on it. Cleo continues, "Oh my God, Pedra, what have I done? What if I'm pregnant by that lunatic?"

CHAPTER TWENTY-SEVEN

"Call me when you get off so that I can go to the pharmacy with you. Even though taking the Plan B pill is pretty cut and dry, I still want to be there for moral support," Pedra says as the ladies walk inside of the building. They head for the elevators.

"Yeah," Cleo mumbles, preparing to go up to her office and confront her man about the shit she just heard. Pedra turns to face her once they step inside of the elevator.

"Promise me that you won't go up there and do something that'll land you in jail." The elevator reaches Pedra's floor and the doors open. She stands in between them to stop them from closing while waiting on a response from Cleopatra. Cleo glares at her friend.

"I can promise you nothing," she replies dryly. Pedra sighs.

"Just call me if you need me. I'll be on standby," she informs her before walking towards the analyst desks. The elevator doors close back and Cleo stares at the floor numbers increasing. She watches the red digits until they reach her level. The doors open slowly.

Cleo gawks at Tava, making Tava feel extremely uneasy. She glares at the woman until she passes her desk. She enters Royal's office just as he's wrapping up a phone call.

"Yes, thank you, Mr. Collins. I'll see you soon." He hangs up with a smile, "Baby, that was the CEO. He wants to meet-"

"You fucking lying asshole!" Cleo shouts at the top of her lungs. Royal looks taken aback.

"Cleo, what-"

"Pedra told me everything, you fucking liar!"

Cleo charges towards Royal in a fit of rage. She swings at him wildly, but he subdues her before she's able to strike a blow. He holds on to her tightly. She wiggles and cries at the same time. He allows her to squirm until she gets tired.

"Are you finished yet?" She's sobbing so hard that she can't answer his question. He looks down at her, "Cleo, please calm down and talk to me. What is going on?"

"You lied to me! You fucking lied!" She whines out. He looks perplexed.

"What are you talking about?"
"You told me you weren't married, Royal, but you fucking are! You fucking lying piece of shit! I hate you!" He lets her go once he hears her words. She beats on his chest like a bongo and he lets her. She pounds away at his pectoral muscles until her emotions get the best of her. She slides down his body, but he catches her before she hits the floor. He holds her up by her waist.

"Baby, I'll tell you everything, I swear, but first, I need you to calm down before you pass out."

Cleo finally stands on her own after getting her breathing together. She leans against his desk, "Royal, I can't fucking believe you! I trusted you-"

"Wait a minute, don't I get a chance to speak my piece before you make up your mind about me?" Cleo doesn't respond, so Royal keeps talking, "Firstly, I want to apologize to you for not filling you in on all of the bullshit that is said around here. I should've told you about the rumors before you heard them from someone else. I guess I was hoping they were dead and buried after all of these years, but I should've known better. Most of these folks weren't even here to experience the shit they think they know so much about. People ain't shit but gossiping ass sheep."

He walks towards the door and locks it. He noticeably takes a deep breath before turning around to face her. He loosens his tie, "Secondly, there was a woman here, Lisa, that I worked closely with. She and I were both analysts back in the day. We were good friends for years and nothing more, and then I got a promotion that landed me in this big ass office with a six-figure salary attached to it. After that, things sort of changed with her. She started flirting with me out of the blue, which was weird because she always told me we'd never be more than friends. Once I moved up in the company, however, she wanted to date all of a sudden. I didn't think anything of it at the time. I swear, I was such a fucking fool back then. Anyway, a few dates later, she was talking about marriage and a family. I was apprehensive at first, but then the thought of having little people eventually grew on me. *She* grew on me."

He walks towards Cleo and grabs her hands. He takes another deep breath before looking into her eyes, "You're right, though. She and I did get married. It was standard and rushed, and it felt wrong from the beginning. After the wedding, her attitude changed completely. She started demanding this lavish lifestyle that frankly, I wasn't interested in at the time. Eventually, she wore me down and I bought her the house, the expensive car, the clothes and jewelry… a bunch of shit that I truly couldn't afford. I tried to make her happy. Unfortunately, she never gave a damn about my happiness. She didn't even like me."

He releases Cleo's hands and proceeds to the window. He gazes out of it, "She never wanted to talk or spend time with me. After she quit this job, she spent most of her days shopping, hanging out, or being on the phone. One day, I decided to follow her and caught her in the arms of another guy. I was completely crushed. All of this shit I was doing for her ass, and she had the fucking audacity to cheat on me with some broke ass chump that didn't even have a car. It turns out he was the dude she'd been dating the whole time she was at Vella Industries. She was simply using me for my money. Anyway, I documented all of my findings and got me the best lawyer that money could buy. Since we had only been married for ten months, I was able to get the marriage annulled. Our union officially never existed. I could finally leave the biggest mistake of my life in the past."

He turns to look at Cleo, "Unfortunately, when you mix business with pleasure, that shit never works out well. No matter how hard I tried to forget about Lisa, this place tried harder to remind me of her."

"So, you never hit her?"

"What! Hit her? Baby, I've never put my hands on a woman in my life. I watched my dad beat my mom and I wanted to kill that bastard! Fuck no."

"Well, what about the baby thing? Tava told Pedra that Lisa was pregnant, but terminated it without your knowledge-"

"Tava said what?"

Royal marches to the door and swings it open before Cleo can respond. Tava looks surprised by his sudden appearance.

"Tava, my office, now!" He shouts. She hesitates to get up from her chair. She crosses the threshold cautiously. Royal slams the door behind her.

"Tava, you have some fucking nerve, you know that?" She looks taken aback.

"Excuse me?"

"You heard me! You're going around telling blatant lies about me and Lisa… why?"

Tava looks as if she can't believe the topic of discussion. She folds her arms in front of her chest before deciding to go there.

"Blatant lies? What blatant lies? You were awful to Lisa and you know it!"

"What the fuck are you talking about? I've never been awful to Lisa! You've never seen me do anything to that woman-"

"I didn't need to! She'd call me all of the time and all I would hear is you yelling, screaming, and calling her names in the background!" Royal looks confused.

"Tava, that's a fucking lie! I never raised my voice at her, not even when I found her at the motel with another man's dick in her mouth!" It's Tava's turn to look confused.

"Another man? She- She never mentioned that-"

"Of course she didn't! Why would she when she was trying to paint this fucked up picture of me?"

Tava doesn't have an answer right away. Royal shakes his head, "And since you want to repeat shit so badly, here's the fucking truth: She and I didn't fuck enough for her to get pregnant. If there was a chance I knocked her up, then she would have made sure I knew about it. That would have guaranteed her gold-digging ass 18 years of steady income. If she did get an abortion, then that means it belonged to that other motherfucker, not me. Either way it goes, though, that shit is in the past, which is right where I should have left your ass. Tava, you're fired."

CHAPTER TWENTY-EIGHT

"Was the security really necessary?" Cleo asks Royal while watching two guards escort Tava to the elevator. He fans his hand in her direction in a dismissive way.

"Man, fuck her. I need everyone to see what happens when you go around trying to sabotage someone else's relationship by spreading a bunch of bullshit that has nothing to do with you." Cleo shakes her head at him before walking inside of their office. He joins her.

"We need to talk."

"I know," he agrees. He closes the door before engaging with her.

"You still lied to me, Royal. You said she was your fiancé, not your wife." He gestures that he knows he was wrong.

"You're right, and I'm sorry, but that bitch doesn't deserve the title of my ex-wife. She is the red in my ledger that I chose to omit. In my defense, when I briefly mentioned her to you, I didn't think you and I would be as close as we are now. I told you, I'm not comfortable opening up to people like that. I had no idea I'd fall head over heels in love with you so quickly… but, here we are." Cleo wants to be upset with Royal, but it's something about his voice that sounds so sincere. She still tries to maintain her attitude, though. *She can't forgive him that easily.*

"How do I know you won't lie to me again?" He grabs her hand gently and places her palm on his chest. The beat of his heart vibrates her fingertips. Their breathing syncs in the connecting moment. They gaze into each other's eyes.

"The only thing I can give you is my word and my heart." Tears form in Cleo's eyes again. Royal's eyes get glossy as well, "Baby, I really hope that's enough, and I promise, I will never lie to you again."

***

Cleo rides Royal like he's wearing a saddle. She works his meat flawlessly, making him moan more than he's comfortable with. His toes curl every time her pussy grinds on his dick. His back arches when he nears his peak. He grabs her ass cheeks firmly.

"Fuck, baby! Fuck!" He swears. Cleo watches his body spasm while she fucks him through his orgasm. He paints her walls white with his cum. She keeps bouncing as if nothing is happening.

"Shit! Slow down, baby! Damn!" He growls. Cleo works her vaginal opening up and down his shaft before easing to a stop. She stares at him until he's able to collect himself. She smirks.

"Don't be tapping out now. Just last week, you were begging for us to keep going." He side-eyes her.

"Whatever. You're talking shit now, but you won't be in a few minutes. I'm about to fuck you so deep that you're going to be running from this dick." Cleo makes a nervous face. He smirks this time, "Nope, don't look stupid now. You just woke up my inner animal, woman. Just give me ten minutes— you're going to be screaming my name."

Royal lifts Cleo off of his lap effortlessly. He stands to his feet and proceeds to the bathroom. Cleo watches his chiseled body until it disappears behind the restroom door. Her phone rings a second later.

"Oh shit," Cleo whispers once she sees the name on her phone screen... *"Pedra"*.

Cleo's first thought is to let it go to voicemail, but she knows Pedra is going to continue calling until she answers. After all, the last time she saw Cleo, Cleo was seriously considering murdering Royal; not to mention the trip Cleo was supposed to be taking to the pharmacy after work for a Plan B pill. Cleo reluctantly answers.

"Hey, girl," she says as normal as possible. Pedra pauses before responding.

"Hey. You never called me, so I was worried about you. How did everything go with Mr. Bradshaw? I didn't see an ambulance, so I figured he's not in the hospital." She giggles, "Were you able to get the pill?"

Cleo takes a deep breath, "You haven't talked to Tava?"

"Talked to Tava? No… why'd you ask me that?"

"Because," Cleo takes another deep breath, "She got fired today."

"What?! Why?"

"Well, Royal didn't appreciate her spreading lies about him and Lisa-"

"Lies? So, he denied being married to her?"

"No. He didn't deny it— Well, technically, he isn't married anymore because he got it annulled, but he did come clean about his and Lisa's relationship. He denied everything else, though."

Pedra's silence deafens Cleo. Cleo cringes up at the thought of her friend secretly judging her. She knows she sounds foolish, but she believes Royal… *whether people call her stupid for it or not.*

"So, it's safe to assume that you didn't get the pill, then, right?"

"You would be right by assuming that, yes," Cleo replies awkwardly. Pedra sighs.

"Cleo, are you sure you know what you're doing?"

"Pedra, please don't go there. You're about to get married to a guy you 'like' just because you mistakenly got pregnant by him. If I don't judge you, then please don't judge me." Pedra smacks her lips.

"Fair enough. So, tell me, will I have a job at the end of the week or will I end up like Tava? I'm almost sure that if Tava's name came up in y'all little argument, then mine came up, too. Is Mr. Bradshaw going to spare me from his wrath?" Pedra's sarcasm gets under Cleo's skin. Cleo rolls her eyes.

"I believe you've been spared this go-round. I would hate for you to lose any sleep over your worries," Cleo spits out, giving Pedra the same amount of sarcasm she's giving her.

"Thank you so much for your concern and thank you for keeping your attack dog off of me. I owe you everything."

The silence between the women contains a strong hint of disgust. Cleo sucks her teeth, "Well, I really should be going now. My man will be back any minute." Pedra hangs up in Cleo's face before she's able to finish her bitchy statement. Cleo sits the phone on the nightstand, *"Fuck you, too."*

CHAPTER TWENTY-NINE

Work has become a place of social anxiety for Cleo. After word got out about Tava being fired because of the gossip she was spreading, people are trying their best to stay out of Royal and Cleo's way. This coming right after Pedra's wedding shower incident doesn't help. Royal and Cleo are quickly becoming the talk of the job, and unfortunately, it's in the worst way possible.

Cleo lets her thoughts get the best of her while staring at the steak on her plate. Royal watches her closely. "Baby, are you OK?" He asks from across the table of the high-end restaurant of his choice. Cleo nods her head.

"Yeah. I'm just a little nervous about this meeting with the CEO tomorrow. Are you sure he's going to be OK with me being there?"

"Of course he will. You're my personal assistant, and personal assistants are allowed at roundtable meetings. I heard he always has his assistant with him." Cleo nods her head again. Royal looks at her curiously, "That was a nice deflection, but really, what's bothering you?"

She takes a deep breath, "It's been nearly a week since you fired Tava and you haven't spoken a word about it. You haven't commented on the cold shoulders the other workers are giving us, or the anonymous complaints about the way you're running the place popping up in the suggestion box." Royal smiles as if she's saying something funny. She folds her arms at his unorthodox reaction, "Babe, I'm serious."

"And that's the problem… you shouldn't be. Everything you're complaining about usually happens to me, anyway. Remember, I've been that building's boss for three years now." She watches him place a piece of ribeye in his mouth. She makes a distraught expression.

"I know, but I'm just saying, you can't fire someone because they were spreading rumors about you. The union will have her back in no time."

"First of all, Tava was never part of the union, she was an at-will employee. Second of all, she was creating a hostile work environment, and she has been for a long time. Her termination paperwork was well-deserved. I should have let her go a long time ago."

Even though Cleo agrees, she still feels bad for Tava. Tava has kids, and now she doesn't have the steady income needed to take care of them. She wishes things could have been different, but sometimes, that's the way the cookie crumbles. Cleo decides to force those thoughts out of her mind. She finally takes a bite of her food.

"So, what do you want to do after we leave here?" Royal wipes his mouth with a napkin before answering her question.

"I did want to go out and see a movie or something, but the longer I'm away from home, the more I want to go back there. I do want to show my lady a good time, though. We've been barricaded in the house the entire weekend." He reaches over and grabs Cleo's hand, "So baby, it's really up to you. This is the last night of freedom we have before we commit ourselves to another week's worth of dirty looks and paperwork. So, what do you think? Rest and relaxation, or a night out on the town?"

***

Even though hanging out sounded like a good idea, Cleo is glad she chose to go back to Royal's place instead.

The two candelabras hold three tall candles each that flicker beautifully on the off-white walls. Cleo and Royal lounge in the jetted tub situated in the middle of one of Royal's bathrooms. The bubbles swallow their bodies from the neck down. They stare at each other lovingly.

"I'm not a mushy person, never have been, but Cleopatra, you make me feel like I want to bear my soul to you." Cleo blushes at Royal's unexpected confession.

"I feel the same way about you, Royal. I can't believe it's been less than a month since I walked into your office for the first time. Who would've thought I'd go from cursing your ass out to being your girlfriend?"

"Me," he admits. "I knew from the moment I saw you that you were going to mean something to me. I just wasn't sure what that something was. Now, I know what it is."

"Oh?" Cleo asks curiously. Royal slides his body towards hers, wrapping his arms around her as soon as he's able to do so. She lays her head on his broad chest. The smell of the coconut oil in her hair fills Royal's nose.

"You're my other half, baby— my twin flame. With you, I feel complete. It's like I've been waiting for you my entire life, but I didn't know that until the very second I saw you. I love you, Cleo. I think I've loved you before I met you. How else would you describe our instant connection?"

Cleo's mouth hangs open in awe. She never thought she'd hear anything as vulnerable as this, especially coming from a man as handsome and established as Royal. She thought she was destined to be alone for the remainder of her life. *Thank the universe she was wrong.*

"Wow, Royal, that was… that was beautiful. I truly don't know what to say," Cleo reveals emotionally. He lifts her chin until his eyes find hers.

"You don't have to say anything but yes."

"Yes?" Cleo asks. Royal produces a ring box from the side of the tub.

"Yes. Cleo…will you marry me?"

***

The 3-carat ring sparkles underneath the ceiling lights. Cleo stares at it as more tears escape her eyes. She stands in front of the kitchen island with a container of orange juice and an empty glass resting near her. The feel of Royal's arms wrapping around her from behind startles her.

"I've been standing in the doorway watching you for the past ten minutes, wondering how long you were going to stand there gawking at your hand," Royal states, squeezing her body tightly. Cleo brushes the tears from her cheeks.

"I'm sorry. I just can't get over how beautiful this ring is. It's breathtaking-"

"Just like you are."

Cleo turns to engage with her new fiancé, "Royal, you don't think we're moving too fast? I mean, we've only known each other for three weeks-"

"Technically, it'll be four weeks tomorrow."

"And we hardly know each other-"

"I know that I love you, and frankly, that's all I need to know."

"But Royal-"

He looks at her strangely, "Why the sudden apprehension? Are you regretting your decision?"

She wraps her arms around his neck, "No! Absolutely not! I don't know… I think I'm in shock. The universe has never been this good to me. My life has been filled with joke after joke and my happiness is usually the punchline. I want to be excited about this, I really do, but every time I get my hopes up, life tends to let me down."

Royal kisses her lips softly, prompting her to calm down instantly. He rests his forehead against hers.

"But what if this is the one time when there are no tricks? No jokes, no punchlines, or any other sinister reasoning? Just good old-fashioned love and happiness? What if we're meant to be and this is the beginning of our happily ever after?" Cleo smiles at the thought.

"You know what, babe? You're probably right."

CHAPTER THIRTY

"Shit, I'm nervous," Royal admits while fixing his tie for the twelfth time. Cleo gives him a caring glare.

"Babe, just relax. You're going to do great," she assures him. They ride the elevator to the top floor, which is a 4,000 square foot office dedicated to the CEO himself. Royal takes a deep breath as soon as the doors open. He walks off first with Cleo directly behind him. They approach the desk of Mr. Collins' secretary. Royal clears his throat.

"Good morning, miss. I'm here for a nine o'clock meeting with Mr. Collins."

The redheaded woman smiles in his direction, "Of course, Mr. Bradshaw. He's expecting you." She stands to her feet, "Right this way."

She leads the duo to a tall set of double doors. She knocks on them before pushing them open."Mr. Collins, your nine o'clock is here," she announces. Royal and Cleo step inside of the massive office. Both of their jaws hit the floor at the sight of the grand space.

"This place is bigger than my apartment," Cleo whispers to Royal. He smiles before facing her.

"You mean your old apartment. I want you to move in with me."

Cleo's face flushes with perplexity at Royal's random request. She quickly wipes the surprise off of her face when Mr. Collins greets them.

"Ahh, Mr. Bradshaw. It's about time I get to put a face with the name," the old white man states with a strong voice. Royal and Cleo walk in his direction once he stands to his feet. Royal sticks his hand out for him to shake.

"Mr. Collins, it's a pleasure to finally meet you."

"Likewise, likewise," he repeats. Royal turns towards Cleo.

"I would like to introduce you to my personal assistant, Cleopatra Strong. She'll be sitting in with us for our meeting. I hope that's OK."

Mr. Collins points to a woman sitting on the couch to his right. She's less than half his age with the body of a supermodel. She slowly stands to her feet.

"And I want to introduce you to my personal assistant, Natasha. Your understudy can stay as long as mine can."

Royal nods his head quickly, "Of course."

"Well then— alright. It's settled, then. The women can linger around while the men handle business."

Mr. Collins' chauvinistic statement rubs Cleo the wrong way, but she decides to let it slide. After all, this is a big deal for Royal. *He's been talking about this meeting nonstop since they woke up this morning.*

Natasha sits next to Mr. Collins while Cleo and Royal sit on the opposite side of his desk. Mr. Collins cuts to the chase, "Mr. Bradshaw, do you know why I requested to meet with you?" Royal looks thrown off by the question.

"Well, per our last conversation, you said you wanted to discuss my excellent work ethic." Mr. Collins gestures that's only partially true.

"Initially, that was my reasoning. Ever since you've been promoted to Senior Manager, things down below have been running like a well-oiled machine. You have the higher-ups very impressed, but there's an incident that has recently come to my attention; an incident of you messily mixing business with pleasure."

Royal glances at Cleo before staring at his boss, "Excuse me?"

Mr. Collins leans back in his seat, "Mr. Bradshaw, can I be completely transparent with you?"

"Yes, please do."

"Alright. I would usually spare the ladies from talk like this, but since this has something to do with them as well, I'll just come right out and say it: It is clearly written in company policy that personal relationships of the intimate kind are not allowed in the same building for obvious reasons. I'm sure you're aware of this."

Royal nods his head that he is, even though Cleo can tell that he isn't. Mr. Collins continues, "So imagine my shock when I found out that you not only married an employee in the past, but now you're smitten with another one." He points at Cleo, "Is it safe to assume that you enjoy shopping for companionship at your place of employment?"

"No! I mean, yes… Sir, it's not like that at all."

"Oh, really? So, the rumors aren't true, then? You aren't dating Ms. Strong?" Royal sighs.

"Yes sir, I am, but I assure you, this isn't some sort of pattern I'm following. Furthermore, my personal relationship with Cleo will not affect my work ethic in any way, shape or form."

"Oh, Mr. Bradshaw— I beg to differ." Mr. Collins reaches into his desk drawer and pulls out a stack of papers. "These are complaints that I've received regarding you and your new assistant. People are claiming they can't locate you after lunch on most days because you've been taking the afternoons off. They also said that you're showing up to employees' functions and making a spectacle of yourself. Oh, and I just caught wind of you firing your secretary for something as juvenile as playground gossip. Does any of this ring a bell?"

Royal looks as if someone took all of the wind out of his sail. He doesn't know how to respond to that. He clears his throat nervously, "Sir, all of that alleged talk is in the past. I'm only concerned with the future of Vella Industries." Mr. Collins chuckles.

"Yes! That's the kind of answer I'm looking for! Spoken like a true leader! Political answers are always the best. Admit to nothing and volunteer nothing. Only speak when absolutely necessary, and never let them see you sweat. If you remember those things, then you'll go far in this company."

Royal nods his head like he's trying to comprehend what just happened. Mr. Collins leans forward with his next words, "Your immediate superior will be retiring at the end of the year, and we really prefer it to be you that takes his position and not some nimrod off of the street. It's a seven-figure gig with a six-figure sign-on bonus. That's not too bad of a deal." Royal smiles at the sound of that. Cleo does, too, "But there's only one requirement, and it's a big one: You have to appear to follow all company policies, including the one about not having personal relationships in the workplace. You can't publicly date your assistant."

Royal and Cleo's eyes go straight to her engagement ring. The CEO notices the diamond distraction as well, "And you definitely can't marry her, not while you both work here."

Royal looks mortified. He glares at his boss with shocked eyes, "So I have to choose between my fiancé and my career?"

"Let me tell you a secret: You see my beautiful assistant? She doubles as my girlfriend, but no one will ever catch wind of that. You can have fun with each other, date, and even fall in love, but you can't get married. At least not until one of you finds another job."

CHAPTER THIRTY-ONE

"I knew it… I knew it… every time I try to be happy…" Cleo sadly mumbles to herself. Whenever things start looking up for her, something always comes along and smashes her dreams. Royal paces their office floor while she wipes the tears from her eyes. She stares at her ring in between her crying spells.

"They can't do this— They can't fucking do this!" Royal shouts. He's so livid that he can throw his desk across the room. He slams down in his seat, "I've worked my ass off for that position, and now they're telling me I can't have it because I want to marry the love of my life? That's bullshit!" The articles on his desk hit the floor after his rage gets the best of him. The noise startles Cleo.

"Royal, you have to calm down."

"How can I, Cleo?" he asks angrily. She walks over to him and places her hand on his shoulder.

"Because, we do have choices here. Not appealing ones, but choices, nonetheless."

"Like?" She wipes the last of her tears away before leaning her backside on his desk in front of him.

"Like me finding another job. It's really no big deal. I can go back to the other building and get my old job back."

"But your pay will be cut in half." She sighs at that ugly fact.

"You're right, but you'll be making a hell of a lot more than you're making now, and since I'm going to be your wife, then that'll be my money, too." She giggles after her partial joke and he does, too. Royal stands to his feet.

"You would really do that for me? You'll let go of six figures just so we can be together?" Cleo nods her head yes.

"I'm doing this for us babe, not just you. It's a chess game, not checkers. This is a no-brainer move. We're sacrificing a hundred grand to make a million. Actually, we shouldn't be crying, we should be celebrating."

He wraps his arms around his lady, "You know what? I love the way you put that, and I think you're right."

***

Cleo contacts Mr. Bernstein to see if her old position is still available. He tells her that it isn't, but he'll make a spot for her anyway because she's one of the best employees he's ever had. He asks her for a little time to move some things around, so she decides to finish the remainder of her work week with Royal. Mr. Bernstein informs her that she'll have a new title first thing Monday morning. She thanks him for looking out for her. Leaving Royal's side is bittersweet, but it's necessary. *It's a small price to pay for a happily ever after.*

After Friday's shift, Royal takes her to a Reggae bar at the edge of town. They spend most of their time dancing the night away. After a couple of hours of vigorous moving, they sit down to rest their sweaty bodies.

"Whew! It got crowded in here quickly, didn't it?" Cleo points out while staring at the sea of people that squeezed into the small space. Royal takes a napkin and wipes his forehead.

"Hell yeah, but it doesn't matter, though. You still danced your ass off out there. Damn, baby! I didn't know you could move like that!"

Cleo licks her lips sexually, "Are you sure you didn't know that?" Royal stands to his feet and moves to her side of the table. He bends down and kisses her so passionately, her toes curl.

"Believe me, I know, and I was hoping you could give me an example of that tonight when we get home."

"You know it," she states with a smile. He smiles back.

"I was thinking about grabbing a drink. You want one?"

"What are you getting?"

"Mm, probably a scotch on the rocks. I hate getting mixed drinks at bars like this. They always find a way to fuck it up."

"You know what? You may be right. I'll just have water, then." Royal makes a surprised face.

"Are you sure? You're not interested in a top shelf Long Island?" Cleo shakes her head no. He pouts, "But baby, I don't want to drink alone."

"You're not. There's 50 other people in here drinking, too." Royal chuckles.

"You're right." He shakes his head, "I'll be right back."

"If you come back and don't see me, I'm in the restroom. I have to go."

Royal gestures that he understands before disappearing into the crowd of happy partiers. Cleo watches him until she doesn't see him anymore. She gets up and proceeds to the bathroom.

"Excuse me… pardon me," she repeats every time she slides past someone. She walks in the stuffed bathroom and jumps in the line for a stall. After ten minutes or so, one finally opens up for her. She walks in and locks the door. She takes a deep breath. Her hand slides inside of her purse, pulling out the box wrapped in plastic as soon as her fingers come across it. She reads the label to herself, *"Early Pregnancy Test"*.

***

Cleo is quiet on the ride home. She can't stop thinking about how drastically things have changed for her over the past month. She never in a million years dreamt she'd be in a relationship with a man that she loves to death…

With a job that changed her tax bracket…

And a positive pregnancy test in her purse…

She's still not sure she believes it.

"Baby, I said we're here. Is everything OK?" Royal asks with a touch of her arm.

"Yes, I'm fine."

"Well, come on, then. I have something I want to give you."

"That's funny— so do I."

Cleo follows Royal to his front door. After walking in the house and removing their shoes, he turns to engage with her.

"Here. I want you to have these," he says, holding a set of keys to his place in front of her face. Cleo covers her mouth with her hand. *She remembers him saying he wanted her to move in, but she didn't think he meant so soon.*

"Royal…what-"

"I've been trying to wait for you to bring up what I said in Mr. Collins' office about you living with me, but you never did."

"I mean, I wanted to, but with everything that's been going on, I didn't think it was vital enough to talk about right now."

He grabs her around the waist, "Anything pertaining to us is of the utmost importance. I want you here with me, baby. Scratch that— I need you here with me. I need to wake up next to you every day. I need to share everything I have with you.”

Royal dangles the keys in front of her face again. Cleo slowly reaches for them with wet eyes. She stares at the keychain attached to them, “C.B.?”

“Yup, your initials. Well, they’ll be your initials as soon as I get you down that aisle.” She kisses him with grateful lips. He happily accepts. She pulls back and stares at the keys in her hand.

“Oh my gosh! I need to start packing! I have so much to do.”

“I know, and I’m not rushing you. You can move your things in here a little at a time until we’re ready to haul everything else over. I’ll be happy to help you prepare. I have no problem with that.”

Cleo kisses Royal again, allowing the smooch to linger a little longer this time. His dick wakes up from their growing lust.

“Wait a minute… before we rip each other’s clothes off, you said you had something to give me as well. So— what is it?” Cleo remembers the pregnancy test inside of her purse. She reaches for it.

“Well, I know you were wondering why I didn’t have a drink at the bar, and I know you’ve noticed that I’ve been a little over-emotional lately, so-”
[DING DONG!]
The sound of someone ringing Royal’s doorbell startles them both. He checks the time on his watch.

“Who the fuck would be coming over my house this time of night?” He fusses. He gasps after looking through the window. He slowly turns to face Cleo, “It’s Lisa.”

CHAPTER THIRTY-TWO

"Well, don't just stand there; open it," Cleo demands with a fold of her arms. Royal swallows hard. He turns to face the door. He takes a deep breath before opening it. Lisa stands there with her arms folded as well.

"Hello, Royal," she spits out dryly. Royal's nostrils flare with fury.

"Lisa, what the fuck are you doing here?" He asks nastily. She smirks.

"Well, since you keep refusing to answer your phone, I thought I'd talk to you in person."

"When you left, I told you to never step foot on my property again."

"Believe me, Royal, I'm not here because I want to be. This visit is strictly business." She looks over his shoulder and spots Cleopatra, causing her to smirk again, "You're really not going to invite me in?"

"Hell no! Whatever you have to say, you can say it on the porch."

Her eyes roll at Royal's rudeness. She reaches in her purse and pulls out a picture. "This is Preston. Isn't he adorable," she questions, holding the photo of a toddler in Royal's eyesight. He barely glances at it.

"Look, my patience is running really thin here, so if you don't make your point in the next ten seconds, then I'm slamming this door in your skanky ass face."

She smacks her lips before pulling out a few sheets of stapled paperwork. She shoves it in his hands. "When I had Preston, I thought he belonged to— well, you know who. It turns out he wasn't the father." She points to the DNA test he's holding. Royal looks bewildered.

"Wait a minute, you had a baby?"

"Anyway, outside of you, he was the only other person I was with, so if he's not the father, then you are."

Cleo and Royal have identical, speechless expressions on their faces. Royal struggles to find his words, "Hold up, back up a second. You had a fucking baby and didn't tell me?"

"Yes, because I thought it was someone else's! Haven't you been listening?" Royal shakes his head in disbelief. Lisa grows impatient with his processing skills. "Look, do we have to keep talking about this outside, or can I come in?" Royal turns to look at a highly distraught Cleo. He steps to the side to let Lisa in. She steps inside and he closes the door. She looks around.

"Wow. This place hasn't changed since I moved out. The house is still decorated the way I left it, I see." She smiles facetiously, "I bet you the bed is still the same, too."

"Excuse you?" Cleo exclaims quickly. Royal steps in and grabs her before she plucks the lace front off of Lisa's head. He tries to calm her down.

"Cleo, can you give us a moment, please? I need to sort this out," Royal requests with a look of distress in his eyes. Cleo looks taken aback.

"You want me to leave while you talk to your ex-wife?"

"No, not leave completely… just step into another room until I hear her out."

"Believe me, sweetie, I don't want his ass. The only thing I'm here for is *our* son."

Lisa stresses the word, "our", causing Cleo to nearly explode. She snatches away from Royal and slides on her shoes. She marches towards the door, "If a moment is what you want, then a moment is what you'll get." She reaches for the doorknob, but Royal stops her.

"Please baby, I don't want you to go." Cleo glares at him as if she could kill him. He takes a step back.

"I need to go. All of a sudden, this place isn't feeling as homely as it once did."

***

Cleo can't sleep, and she's not sure if it's because of the cold, hotel bed, or the fact that Royal has been calling her phone nonstop. After fleeing from Royal's home, she was so distraught that she could barely drive. She decided to stop at the first hotel she saw. She paid for a room for the weekend, even though she wasn't sure if she was going to be there the entire time. She needed to think, and she needed to do it somewhere where Royal couldn't easily find her.

She rolls over on the tear-stained pillow and reaches for her cell. She powers it off after it stops ringing for the 17th time. She tosses it back on the nightstand.
"What am I going to do?"

She lays on her back and rubs her abdomen. She can't believe she's going to be a mom for the first time this late in her life. She can't believe she thought that her and Royal were going to share the same sentiments, only to find out that he already has a baby with an ex-wife that he claimed was just his fiancé. *"Cleo, what have you gotten yourself into?"*

She needs to talk to someone about this, but she hasn't spoken to Pedra since she hung up in Cleo's face. Royal has been Cleo's best friend lately, but now he's public enemy number one. At first, she was sad about leaving her personal assistant position, but now she couldn't be happier. Not having to be around Royal or Pedra is the only thing that'll make her feel better. *Out of sight, out of mind.*

Cleo is finally able to drift off to sleep. A nightmare about her walking in on Lisa and Royal having sex wakes her. Tears stream down her puffy face. She finds herself in the bathroom on her knees vomiting out her sorrows.

"Cleo! Thank God!" She hears from behind her. She turns her head suddenly to find Royal standing in the restroom's doorway. She glances down at the key card in his hand.

"How'd you find me?" She asks before getting off of the floor. She heads to the sink.

"We share phone locations, remember? I've known where you were since you left. I wanted to give you space, but when you turned your phone off, I got worried." He wants to approach her but figures it's best to keep his distance. He opts to watch her wash out her mouth instead.

"But how did you get a key?" She follows up. She stares at him through the mirror. He makes eye contact with her reflection.

"I told the dude at the front desk that I was your husband and that I left mine in the room."

"You're still lying, I see." She turns around to face him, "The only wife you've ever had was Lisa. Where is she, by the way? Making herself at home at the place she decorated, Mr. 'Those unknown calls are spam calls, not my ex blowing my shit up'?"

Royal makes a face as if he doesn't know what to say. Cleo storms past him. She's sitting on the edge of the bed by the time he finds the courage to face her.

"Cleo, we need to talk." She cuts her eyes at him.
"So do it. Talk."

"First, I want to start off by saying that I had no idea she had a baby— like none. I need you to hear me on that."

"I hear you," she interjects quickly. He nods his head before easing down on the bed, "Second, I heard her out, and I told her that I'm not seeing this child or entertaining the thought of him being mine until I get a DNA test."

"As you should," she adds. He fiddles with his fingers nervously.

"Third, I still want you to move in with me, baby. I really need you-"

She holds her hand up to silence him. She turns to gawk at him with a serious gaze. "Did she pick that house out?" He sighs loudly before answering.

"Yes. She did."

"And she decorated it, too, correct?"

"Yes."

"And that's the same bed you were fucking her in, right?"

"Cleo, come on. That's not fair." She puts her hand up again.

"Fine. That's fine. You don't have to answer that." She takes a deep breath, "Well, I'm sorry, Royal, but I refuse to move into you and another bitch's house."

"But baby! That house is brand fucking new! I have a thirty-year contract on that property-"

"And that's fine. I'm not telling you to move, I'm telling you that I can't live there… sorry."

Royal stands to his feet and paces the floor. He takes a deep breath to calm his growing frustrations with her. "Baby, listen, be level-headed about this. So what, she picked out the house? And? It's just a shell! We can gut it and decorate it any way you'd like. I need my future wife to share my space with me."

"You mean with you and your son?"

"Dammit, Cleo! Would you stop! As of this very moment, I don't have any kids!" Cleo stands to her feet, too. She places her hand over her womb.

"Sorry, but you're wrong again, Royal. You do have at least one... I'm pregnant."

CHAPTER THIRTY-THREE

"You're pregnant?" Royal repeats in a shaky voice. Cleo doesn't respond, realizing that she can't say those words again without getting emotional. Royal rushes to her side, "Oh my God! Baby, you're having my baby?" He places his hand over hers. She tries her best to maintain her angered state, but the overwhelming situation is getting the best of her. She begins weeping suddenly. Royal wraps his arms around her.

"Baby, I'm so sorry," he whispers while she cries loudly on his chest. He holds her lovingly, kissing her forehead every few seconds to let her know he's there for her. She pulls herself together eventually. He helps her sit down and gets on his knees in front of her.

"100 times, I'm sorry. I never, ever wanted to hurt you. I never wanted to put you through any of this."

"You've been lying to me nonstop, Royal! We've only been together for a month and you've been lying to me the entire time!" Royal wipes away the newest tears streaming down Cleo's distraught face. He covers her hands with his.

"I know I've been a shitty boyfriend, but I didn't know how to tell you about her. I love you, baby, and like I promised you before, I will never lie to you again. Never. You have my word. Whatever you want to know, I'll tell you. Just please, don't pull away from me— not right now. I don't think I'll be able to handle it."

The tears trickling down Royal's face touches Cleo in the deepest part of her heart. She decides to return the favor and brushes away his tears as well. He pulls her body closer to his and kisses her softly. They make out in that position until the intimate gesture starts to mend Cleo's broken heart. He backs her towards the pillow. He stares into the depths of her eyes.

"I've never felt this way about anyone before, and I'm sure I never will again. I will do everything it takes to keep you by my side, and now that you're having my baby, I will do anything to make sure you're happy."

Cleo grins at the gesture, "Anything?" He nods his head.

"Yes, anything."

"Good, because I'm starving. I would really love it if we got something to eat."

***

Instead of the couple going to one of their respective homes, they decide to stay at the hotel that Cleo was initially using to hide from Royal. He upgrades their room to the best suite the establishment has. Now, they're pigging out on pizza, wings, and cupcakes while watching a rom-com.

Royal belches, "Damn baby, I'm stuffed. I don't think I can take another bite." Cleo balls her face up at his lack of manners.

"Excuse you! And nobody told you to try to eat the whole damn pizza, anyway. You claimed you didn't even want any." He smiles before unbuttoning his jeans.

"I didn't before I saw it. That shit looked good." Cleo smacks her lips at him before shoving him in the arm. He smiles.

"Well, you better slow down, greedy. We both can't be fat. I'm the one that's pregnant, not you." Royal leans up and kisses her lips, just like he does every time Cleo mentions her condition. He gawks at her in amazement.

"I get goosebumps every time you say that shit. I fucking love you, woman." Cleo laughs.

"You know what? Something is wrong with you, Royal Bradshaw."

"And do you know what? You're the one thing that's right with me, soon to be Cleopatra Bradshaw." She blushes.

"Oh, shut up. I love you, too."

The kissing starts that usually leads to Royal's dick sliding inside of Cleo. He lays her body across the couch gently, climbing between her legs like that's where he belongs. Their clothes take turns hitting the floor. Royal's cell phone rings before he gets the chance to enter her.

"Dammit! Who the fuck?" He exclaims while climbing off of her. He answers the phone as soon as he reads the screen.

"Hello?... Yes, that's correct... Great! I'll be down there first thing tomorrow morning... Thanks for all of your help... Goodbye."

Royal takes a deep breath after ending the call. He looks in Cleo's direction, "That was my lawyer. He found a lab that'll do the DNA test for me and Lisa's son. We all have to report to the diagnostics place in the morning.

"On a Sunday?"

"Yeah. The quicker I can get this done, the better."

"Oh...OK," Cleo mumbles, trying her best not to sound as uncomfortable as that information made her feel. She sits up and covers her nude body with Royal's shirt. He hesitates on his next statement.

"I- I need to call Lisa to let her know where to meet me in the morning."

"That's fine," Cleo states.

"I can call her in front of you if you'd like-"

"No, go ahead. You can have your privacy."

Cleo is looking at Royal so blankly that he can't tell if she's being facetious or not. He decides to call Lisa on the spot. *Fuck that, he's not taking any chances.*

"Yeah, this is Royal… I'm calling to let you know that my lawyer found a spot for us to do the DNA test tomorrow morning… Right, a place called Vella Diagnostics… I'm sure you do know exactly where it is… Calm the fuck down, I'm not trying to say anything! Look, just meet me up there at eight in the morning and bring your son." Royal hangs up with a grind of his teeth. Cleo watches his anger grow, and then dissipate. He rejoins his lover on the couch.

"I'm sorry about that, baby. That bitch really gets under my skin," he mutters. Cleo rubs his arm.

"I've been meaning to ask you— Do you think her son is yours?" Royal eases back on the couch with a deep sigh. He wipes his face with both hands.

"I mean, I don't know. His age does fit with our marriage, and he does sort of look like my family, but all of that is subjective. Even though she says she's positive I'm his father, I'm sure she said that to the other guy, too. She's such a liar and a cheater that she could have easily been with way more guys than just me and him. The only way to know for sure is to do the test." Cleo gestures that she agrees.

"How long will the results take?"

"It's a rapid test, so I'll know in 24 to 48 hours."

Cleo's eyes react to the news, "Wow, that's really quick."

"Yeah," he agrees. The atmosphere is filled with uneasy awkwardness. Royal turns his naked body towards Cleo, "So, where were we?"

"Somewhere that I'm not in the mood to revisit right now," Cleo replies dryly. She reaches for her panty, but he stops her.

"I'm so sorry to hear that. I guess I'm going to have to eat your pussy until you feel like revisiting it again." Royal gets down on all fours. He drapes one of Cleo's legs over his shoulder. His fingers part her labia, exposing her pink clit from underneath its hood. He licks his lips at the thought of sucking on it.

"I thought you were full?" She asks flirtatiously.

"Oh no, baby, I'm never too full for you. I'm a glutton for your sweet nectar."

CHAPTER THIRTY-FOUR

Cleo sees Royal off first thing in the morning. She acts like all of this DNA test business is cool with her, but in all actuality, it makes her sick to her stomach. Cleo's baby was supposed to be Royal's first baby, not that gold-digging whore of an ex he has. She prays to all of the powers that may be for Royal not to be the father of Lisa's son. This can't be how they start their lives together. *This can't be their happily ever after.*

Royal arrives back to the room a few hours after he leaves. He's toting breakfast food from a local restaurant. Cleo smiles when he comes through the door, even though she's not in the mood to do so. He puts on a fake smile as well.

"Hey, baby," he greets her, carrying the food to the table in front of the couch. He sits the bag on top of the old food boxes from yesterday. Cleo joins him.

"Hey," she says, kissing him quickly on his lips. They try their best to ignore the awkwardness between them, even though it's growing more noticeable every second. Royal sits on the couch.

"I brought you an omelet with the works, and an apple juice," he points out. He opens the Styrofoam container he assumes is hers. She instantly covers her nose.

"Oh my God, that smells awful," she exclaims, running towards the bathroom after her words. Royal looks perplexed once Cleo starts to vomit in the toilet. He proceeds to check on her.

"Damn, baby. I'm sorry. I didn't mean to make you sick." Cleo wipes her mouth with the back of her hand.

"It's not your fault. Well, this pregnancy is, but not that food smelling absolutely rancid," she says jokingly. She cleans her face and mouth at the sink. Royal stares at her curiously.

"So, you being pregnant is my 'fault'?" He uses air quotes to seriously question her. She turns and looks at him strangely.

"Well, it was your constant begging to let you cum in me that got me knocked up. You know I wasn't that interested in having a baby."

Royal looks offended, "My constant begging? So, I was begging you?" Cleo opens her mouth to respond, but he cuts her off to continue his rant, "And you're not interested in having a baby? So, what exactly does that mean? Are you planning on being a shitty mom or something? If so, then we can make arrangements for my child to be raised by me-"

"Hold on… what the fuck did you just say? Are you threatening to take my baby from me?" Royal wants to continue digging the hole that he's quickly finding himself in, but he bites his tongue. Angry tears gush from Cleo's wowed eyes. *When did their conversation take such a rapid turn for the worse?*

"Look, I get you're upset about all of this shit going on with your ex, but that doesn't give you the right to pick on me! You know you wanted this baby more than I did, but that doesn't mean I'm going to love our child any less! You're completely out of fucking line, Royal, and I don't think I want to be around you right now!"

Cleo bumps past him. He grabs her by the arm, "Baby… wait. You're right," he confesses sadly. Cleo wipes her eyes before giving him the satisfaction of acknowledging his words. He expels a deep breath, "I was trying to be OK with all of this. I was trying my best to keep it together at that damn diagnostics place today, but when I saw her son…" tears build up in his eyes, "When I saw him, I just knew he was mine."

His words knock the wind from Cleo's chest. Her face reacts to the shocking news. Royal eases down on the bed depressingly. Cleo joins him with her bottom lip dragging the floor. Her throat burns with her next question, "How did you know?"

"Looking at him was like looking at one of my baby pictures. He's me at two. It was so uncanny that I snapped a picture of him and sent it to my mom. After she cosigned my feelings, I knew he had to belong to me."

Cleo can't listen anymore. Her stomach hurts violently. She hurries to the bathroom once more, painting the toilet water with the pain of Royal's words. She heaves until nothing comes out. She curls up on the cold bathroom floor once she notices that throwing up didn't offer her an ounce of relief. Royal rushes to her side.

"Baby! What's wrong? What can I do?" He asks frantically. Her face squinches from the excruciating pain while she holds her abdomen.

"Help me get dressed and take me to the hospital. Something's wrong."

***

"Ms. Strong, how are you feeling?" The female doctor asks after entering her room. Cleo sits up in the hospital bed before responding.

"Better. I don't know what's in this IV, but it works wonders." The physician grins.

"It's just a little cocktail for pregnant women we whipped together. Some fluids, nutrients, and a hint of pain meds. No alcohol, I promise." Both women giggle, but Royal's concern stops him from joining in on the light-hearted laughter.

"My apologies for not being in a chuckling mood, but I would really like to know how the baby is doing? She was having bad stomach pains before we got here. I thought something was wrong." The doctor nods her head as if she understands.

"I'm sorry, sir. Let me address your questions and concerns right now." She glances at the clipboard in her hand, "There's a couple of things I want to talk to you about; Mainly, prenatal care. Is it true that you have yet to visit an OB/GYN?"

"That's correct. I just found out I was pregnant two days ago. I haven't had time to fully process the news."

"I completely understand, but I have to tell you how important it is that you start prenatal care as soon as possible. Unfortunately, black women that are your age and weight have the greatest risk of pregnancy issues, birthing problems, and infant defects. I don't want to scare you, I just want you to be as safe and as prepared as possible."

"So, what about now? Is my baby OK now?" Cleo questions in an alarmed tone.

"Yes. Everything seems to be just fine. Your amniotic sac is in a great spot, and it's the normal size for this stage of your pregnancy."

"Seems to be fine? Why aren't you surer than that?" Royal wonders worriedly.

"Well, it's too early in Ms. Strong's pregnancy for us to see the embryo. She has to wait a week or two before the developing fetus is big enough to be seen on a sonogram."

Royal and Cleo nod their heads as if they're trying to process the doctor's words. She smiles at the couple warmly, "Don't get yourself worked up too much over the what-ifs. This is a wonderful and magical time for you both. Bond over the upcoming moments, enjoy your pregnancy. Share this experience together. It's really great." Royal grabs Cleo's hand and squeezes it lovingly.

They share an intimate moment once their eyes meet. The doctor clears her throat to reclaim their attention, "And please, Ms. Strong, try your best to relax. Stress is like poison to a pregnancy, especially one as high-risk as yours. I want you to take it easy, no matter what. Stay away from stressful situations! That goes for you, too, sir."

CHAPTER THIRTY-FIVE

Cleo isn't sure why, but her first day back at the old office gives her heavy anxiety. She tries not to overthink it, mainly because the doctor warned her against getting too excited. Too much emotion in either direction can cause her pregnancy complications, and the last thing she wants to do is jeopardize the well-being of her and Royal's child.

Cleo feels a huge sense of relief thanks to all of the friendly faces that seem happy to see her. Things were so hostile when she worked with Royal that she forgot how it feels to truly enjoy her work environment. A few familiar coworkers stop her for a quick chat. Her mood grows better with every positive interaction. She starts to breathe a little easier. She's smiling by the time she approaches Mr. Bernstein's office.

"Ahh… Cleopatra! It's so nice to have you back!" Her boss says as soon as she enters his personal space.

"It's so nice to be back. Thank you for creating a spot for me. I really appreciate you moving things around."

"Oh, it was no big deal. I just can't believe you gave up that six-figure salary to come back here! Tell me— did they fill that position yet, or are they still hiring? I wouldn't mind putting in an app." Cleo giggles at his joke and so does he.

"I know it sounds crazy, but things got a little too complicated over there. It was good while it lasted, though." Mr. Bernstein glances at the rock on her wedding finger. His eyes react to its luxurious gleam.

"I'd say. If that's what a complication looks like, then sign me up!" They both laugh again. Cleo shakes her head amusingly.

"You know what, Mr. Bernstein? I've missed your terrible sense of humor."

"And I miss you being around to laugh at it. It usually makes my wife want to strangle me." He humps his shoulders. Cleo shakes her head again.

"So, where am I working now?" He glances down at a sheet of paper on his desk.

"Actually, I'm waiting on one more new employee before I take you to your floor. She's supposed to be here-" he pauses when someone behind Cleo catches his eye, "Never mind. I see her coming right now."

Cleo follows his gaze. Her mouth hangs open at the sight of the familiar female. The woman looks at Cleo the same way. She steps next to her.

"Hello, Cleopatra."

"Hello, Tava."

***

The ladies follow Mr. Bernstein to the elevator. They take it up a few levels. After the doors open, Cleo notices the layout looks very similar to the floor Royal works on in his building. Mr. Bernstein leads them to an office door that resembles Royal's office door as well. He turns around to face the women before proceeding further.

"One of my Processing Technicians recently got promoted to Senior Manager. He's in serious need of two assistants, or two secretaries, or hell— whatever he feels he needs; and I thought since you both have experience with the Senior Manager at the other building, you could help him get acclimated." Cleo and Tava glance at each other awkwardly.

"What about the pay? Will the pay resemble the pay we received when we worked for the other Senior Manager?" Cleo questions.

"There's no six-figure salary if that's what you're asking," Mr. Bernstein informs her. Tava cuts her eyes at Cleo as if she didn't know she was making that much.

"So, what is the salary amount, then?"

"You'll have to ask him that."

Mr. Bernstein knocks on the door. After hearing a response, he opens it. The man sitting behind the desk stands to his feet. Cleo grits her teeth at the sight of the unfriendly face, but he smirks when he sees hers. She folds her arms unpleasantly. Mr. Bernstein fails to notice their tension.

"Cleo, I'm not sure if you remember Anthony— or Mr. Matthews as he goes by now." Pedra's ex joins them near his office's entrance while Mr. Bernstein introduces him. Cleo sucks her teeth.

"Yes, I remember him," she spits out. He sticks his hand out for her to shake. She does so quickly.

"And this is Tava. She comes highly recommended from the Downtown office."

"Highly recommended?" Cleo whispers to herself. *"How can someone that got fired be highly recommended?"*

Anthony greets her the same way he greeted Cleo. Tava shakes his hand with a smile. Mr. Bernstein takes a step backwards.

"Alrighty… I wish I could stay, but unfortunately, I have a processing floor to run. Congratulations again, Anthony, and ladies, good luck." Everyone bids their farewells before Mr. Bernstein disappears from their sights. Anthony rubs his hands together in an exciting way.

"Hell yeah! I get assistants and shit! This is going to be fun."

*****

Tava sets up her belongings at the secretary's desk while Cleo sets up hers at the assistant's desk. There is no divider in Anthony's office like there is in Royal's, so privacy is not an option. She tries to ignore Anthony's constant stares, but eventually, they get under her skin. She finally meets his eyes with hers.

"Is there a problem?" Cleo exclaims nastily. Anthony chuckles at her typical outburst.

"Damn, Cleo. Are you still mad at me for the way things went down with Pedra?" Cleo narrows her eyes at him. Even though she and Pedra aren't on speaking terms right now, that's still her homegirl. Anthony had no business treating her the way he did. *He's the scum of the fucking Earth.*

"Hell yeah I am, and always will be! You mistreated the shit out of her with your lying ass! How is your wife doing, by the way? Has she forgiven you for carrying on a work relationship for two years yet?"

Anthony's jaw tightens at the mention of his drama-ridden past. He takes a deep breath before addressing her snippy concern, "Actually, no, my ex-wife never forgave me for my infidelity— hints the word, 'ex'. I've been single ever since the divorce."

"Good. A no-good asshole like you needs to be single." Anthony huffs.

"Ok, Cleo. Get it all out of your system. All of the hateful things you want to say, all of your smart-ass remarks... whatever it's going to take for us to move past this shit. Pedra has already forgiven me for what happened between her and I-"

"How would you know what Pedra has forgiven you for? Just because she has moved on doesn't mean she's over what you did to her-"

"Knock! Knock!" The sound of someone's voice from outside of the office door stops Cleo in mid rant. She and Anthony stare in its direction as it opens, "I see my girl, Tava, is your new secretary. I'm glad my recommendation paid off-"

Pedra stops talking when her eyes land on Cleo. Both women freeze as if they've spotted a ghost. Anthony glares at Cleo amusingly, "Now, what were you saying about Pedra not forgiving me again?"

CHAPTER THIRTY-SIX

"Cleo— What are you doing here?" Pedra has to ask. Cleo is the last person she thought she'd find in Anthony's office. *Cleo feels the same way about Pedra.*

"I was just about to ask you the same thing," Cleo admits shockingly. Pedra lets go of the door, allowing it to close behind her.

"Well… I was just— I mean, I had to— I decided to check on Tava on my way to work," she lies. Cleo smacks her lips at her attempt to insult her intelligence.

"Really, Pedra?" Pedra lets out a heavy sigh.

"Can we talk about this somewhere else?" Cleo stands to her feet.

"Sure. Lead the way."

The women quietly head towards the women's bathroom. As soon as they're inside, Cleo impatiently breaks their silence, "I thought you and Anthony were beefed out?!"

"We were! But after you told me Tava lost her job, I felt obligated to help her find another one. After all, I was the one that told you what she said about Mr. Bradshaw. If I would have kept her name out of it, then she would've still been employed. So, I decided to call Mr. Bernstein to see if they had any openings at this building. He told me about Anthony's new position. He said he thought Ant needed a secretary but he wasn't sure, so he suggested that I give him a call. The conversation between Ant and I started off strictly business, I swear, but then we started to reminisce about our relationship. We reminisced for nearly six hours. We- We've been talking every day since."

Pedra makes an uneasy face with her last statement. Cleo wants to challenge her friend's sanity but decides not to go there. With her making questionable choices herself lately, she has no room to criticize Pedra's decision-making skills. *That'll be the pot calling the kettle black.*

"So, what does that mean exactly? Are things still going well with Connor?"

"As good as can be expected." Pedra's face grows even more uneasy. Cleo places her hand on Pedra's shoulder.

"I know things haven't been that friendly between us lately, but you know you can always talk to me, right?" Pedra's eyes gloss over with emotion. Cleo can tell Pedra wanted to reach out to her just as badly as she wanted to reach out to Pedra. Pedra brushes a tear from her cheek.

"You were right about me, you know? I guess that's why your words stung so bad. I am marrying Connor because I'm pregnant, not because he and I are a good fit. Would I have a decent life with Connor? Probably, but would I be happy?" Pedra pauses as if she's afraid to answer her own question. Cleo decides to interject her personal issues to give Pedra a mental break from her own.

"You were right about me, too. I did jump into this thing with Royal way too soon. I should have pumped the brakes and truly got to know him and his baggage before fully committing to his ass."

"Committing to him?" Pedra inquires, catching a glimpse of Cleo's engagement ring. Surprise fills her eyes. "Shit, Cleo! Oh my gosh! Your ring is gorgeous! It's massive!" She expresses in a shocked tone. She grabs Cleo's hand to get a better look at it. She can't help but to compare it to hers. Envy floods her eyes.

"Thanks. It is beautiful," Cleo mumbles in an unenthused way. Pedra looks concerned.

"But I thought this is what you wanted? You have a guy you really care about that can afford that house on the hill you've always dreamt of. The only thing you're missing is a baby and an expensive ass dog." Cleo's face is uneasy this time. Pedra reads it perfectly, "Hold on— Don't tell me you're…"

Cleo nods her head to confirm the pregnancy inquiry Pedra is trying to get out of her mouth. Pedra hugs her without warning, "Oh my God! This is so fucking dope! My best friend and I are pregnant together!" Pedra is ecstatic until she notices that Cleo isn't. Pedra releases her with a weird expression on her face, "OK… Clearly, I'm missing something."

"Yeah… a lot."

"Well, I'm listening."

Cleo tells Pedra about Lisa popping up on Royal's doorstep and pinning her son on him. She also mentions her reasoning for working with Anthony and Royal's new job offer. Then, she tells her about her high-risk pregnancy and how much the delicate situation scares the shit out of her. Pedra genuinely listens to her friend, handing her tissues to wipe her tears when needed. She rubs Cleo's arm gently.

"Everything is going to be OK, Cleopatra, trust me. It sounds like Royal really loves you and is going to do right by you and your child, and I'll always be here to support you. We can support each other." Cleo finds a grin amongst her tears.

"Thanks, Pedra. That means a lot. It's just— if this test comes back and Royal is the father, I don't know what I'll do."

"I'm not sure, either, but I can tell you what you're not going to do: You're not going to stress that baby out of you, that's for damn sure." Cleo takes a deep breath. *Pedra is right.*

"I agree with you, but you have to promise me that you won't get stressed, either. I know getting married can work a person's nerves, but in a couple of weeks, you can put all of that behind you. You'll officially be Connor's wife."

Pedra breaks eye contact with Cleo. She plays with her engagement ring awkwardly before slowly sliding it off of her finger. She stares at it like she's never seen it before, "I don't know if there's going to be a wedding anymore."

"What? What do you mean?"

"Well, like I said, Connor and I aren't a good fit. After you and I talked at the restaurant that afternoon, your words have been running through my mind ever since. You told me to live for myself, not my family, and that I shouldn't marry Connor just because I'm pregnant."

Cleo nods her head, letting Pedra know she remembers the conversation. Pedra continues, "I knew I didn't really want to be with Connor, but I felt trapped. I don't know how to raise a baby, and I'm terrified to do so on my own. I only said yes to him out of fear of being a single mom."

"So, what changed then?"

"Anthony. Having one conversation with him reminded me of what I would be missing if I settled for Connor. Anthony awakens something within me; he makes me feel alive— just like he did when we were together back then."

Pedra pauses out of fear of being judged. Cleo doesn't react negatively to the news, so Pedra decides it's safe to keep talking, "I know he's made mistakes, but it seems like he's learned from them. I really think he and I have a real shot at making our relationship work this go-round."

"But Pedra, you're pregnant. Did you tell him about the baby?"

"I did, and he said it didn't matter, that he wanted to be with me, anyway. He said he loved me, and he'd love my baby, too. He wants to raise my baby as his own, and I think I'm going to let him do it."

CHAPTER THIRTY-SEVEN

"Pedra…wow," is the only thing Cleo can get out of her mouth at the moment. She stares at her friend and reads the seriousness on her face. "Well, what do you plan on telling Connor?" Pedra humps her shoulders.

"That's the problem; I have no fucking idea."

"But you guys are getting married in what? Two weeks from now? Everyone has their dresses and suits for the wedding, not to mention the plane tickets that your family and friends have already purchased-"

"I know, I know. I keep going over everything in my head. Me calling this wedding off will affect and disappoint a lot of people, and Connor… Connor is going to be heartbroken."

"Exactly," Cleo agrees.

"But what's the alternative? Me going through with a wedding that I know is a mistake? Going through all of the legalities of this thing just to dismantle it later? Break Connor's heart then instead of now?"

"OK, I get the 'calling off the wedding' part, but do you really believe he's going to allow another man to raise his child?"

"Not if I tell him the baby isn't his."

"Pedra, no! You wouldn't!"

"I don't know, Cleo… I think I would."

Pedra has done a lot of questionable things in her life but ripping a child from its paternal side of the family will be an all-time low. Cleo wants to tell her friend how extremely terrible that idea is but decides to stay out of it.

Pedra's life. Pedra's choice. Pedra's karma.

Pedra shakes her head at her own messy predicament, "I'm already going to be considered a cold-hearted bitch for calling off the wedding, so I might as well go all the way for the jugular. I want to be free from Connor once and for all, and this is the only way I can think of to do it."

***

Royal coerces Cleo into coming over to his place after work, even though she really doesn't want to do so. She hasn't walked through his front door since finding out his residence was more of his ex-wife's home than his. She takes a deep breath before using her keys to enter his house. She's surprised to find the place completely empty.

"Royal!" She shouts out before kicking off her shoes. He appears from the kitchen doorway a few seconds later. A big smile covers his face as he approaches her. He hands her one of the two wine glasses in his hands.

"Royal, you know I can't have this," Cleo informs him in an annoyed tone. He rolls his eyes before pecking her on the lips.

"Do you really think I'd give you wine while you're carrying my seed? Absolutely not."

"So, what is it then?"

"Sparkling grape juice. We had to toast with something."

"OK… so we're toasting to something— which is what?"

"Uh, isn't it obvious?" He states, spinning around in a circle. "We're toasting to new beginnings. I took today off and donated almost everything in this house to charity…and yes, that included the bed." He gives her a goofy look. She smiles, "I really want you to feel comfortable here, baby. I really want this house to be about us and our family."

Cleo's smile fades after hearing the word "family". It reminds her that she's still holding her breath regarding Royal's DNA test results. He reads the pain in her eyes.

"Baby, listen to me. No matter what that test says, you and I are forever. You and our child will be my top priority… always." He kisses her again. She takes a step away from him.

"I know, and I love you Royal, but I just need time to process all of this. It's a lot."

"I know it is, baby, and the last thing I want to do is stress you out and harm our child, so whatever it is you need me to do, I'll do it. If you need space, then I'll back off. Just let me know."

Cleo looks troubled after his words. She wants Royal to give her space, but she doesn't want him to miss a single second of her pregnancy. She places her hand on her developing embryo. He watches her, having the strong urge to touch her midsection as well.

"Royal, I need you— we need you, but I think it's best for me to stay at my apartment a little longer… just until we get to the bottom of this stuff with your ex and brainstorm some design ideas for redecorating. I want everything to be right." He nods his head in agreement, even though he doesn't fully agree.

"Ok, baby. Whatever you want. Can we at least look at a few color samples so I can get the painters out here? I need to keep myself busy with something to stop myself from missing you." She blushes before walking up to drape her arms around his neck.

"You better miss me! And who says you can't come over and visit? Just because we're not moving in with each other this very second doesn't mean we're not going to spend time with each other. If I have to go through the physical motions of being pregnant, the least you can do is be around to hear about it."

"I'm definitely going to be around; not as often as I'd like, but I'll settle for whatever time I can get." Cleo smacks her lips before pressing them against his. They make out for the first time since Royal visited Vella Diagnostics. Things get hot and heavy between them in record time. Royal slides his hand underneath Cleo's skirt and between her thighs, going straight for her pleasure spot. Her legs vibrate at the feel of his warm fingertips rubbing her clit through her moistening panty. Her knees buckle from the arousing moment.

"Damn, babe. Now I wish you would've kept the bed," Cleo confesses sexually. Royal smiles with a bite of his lip.

"I don't. If I never would've gotten rid of that old bed, then that new state-of-the-art sleeper upstairs wouldn't have been delivered this morning." Cleo's eyes grow wide with excitement. She hurries towards the staircase. Royal watches her curiously, "Baby, where are you going?"

"To the bedroom. If there's a new bed upstairs, then what are we still doing down here? We should've been up there breaking that sucker in."

CHAPTER THIRTY-EIGHT

Cleo's exiting the shower when she hears Royal's phone ring. He talks on it briefly, ending the call before she makes it to his bedroom. His knee is shaking with nervousness while he sits on the edge of the bed. Cleo places her hand on his shoulder.

"Babe, what is it?" She asks with concern. The sound of Royal's cell chiming directs their attention towards it. He presses on the envelope icon on its screen, which directs him to his email account. He takes a deep breath before reading over the urgent message.

"Fuck!" He shouts, throwing the expensive phone against the wall. The sound of it breaking startles Cleo. He wipes his face hard before standing to his feet. Angry pacing immediately follows. He clears the tears that are trying to escape his eyes. Cleo approaches him cautiously.

"Babe— please, talk to me," she requests. Royal is so angry, he can burst.

"That bitch! That fucking bitch!" He shouts. Cleo grabs her stomach, reminding herself to stay calm no matter what Royal is about to say.

"What- What is it?" She stutters.

"That was my lawyer. He called to let me know that the DNA test results were in." Cleo's heart drops to the hollowest part of her chest. She tries to swallow the lump forming in her throat. She takes a few breaths before furthering the conversation.

"OK… so what did they say?" Royal stops pacing to stare at his lady. The look of utter defeat in his eyes nearly brings her to her knees. Her butt finds the bed before she's able to collapse completely.

"No," she mutters, allowing her tears to roll towards her chin. They gather and then fall on the towel she has wrapped around her body. Royal wants to comfort her, but he can barely hold himself together. He sits on the bed next to her.

"He sent the results via email… 99.97% probability of paternity."

Cleo stares straight ahead. She can't bring herself to look at Royal. Even though this baby was made before she knew Royal existed, she still feels like he betrayed her. How is she supposed to find the strength to be OK with this? How is their relationship going to work now that he officially has another child besides theirs?

"Baby— please— I- I need you right now. Please don't shut down on me. Please," Royal begs with tears trickling down his cheeks. Cleo shakes her head slowly like she's not sure what to do.

"Royal, I- I can't," she mumbles. He places his hand over hers.

"Please, Cleo, don't do this."

"Do you love me?" Royal looks offended by the question.

"Of course I love you."

"And do you love our unborn child?"

"Baby, of course I do."

"Then you will understand me when I tell you that I can't do this right now. If I try to deal with this at this very second, then the stress will send me back to the hospital, and I don't want to go through that again." Royal expels a deep sigh.

"And I don't want you to go through that again, either." He unhurriedly slides his hand off of hers. She stands to her feet.

"I think you should talk to your family about this… maybe call your mom. She'd be happy to hear she has a grandson," Cleo suggests in a hurt tone. She walks towards Royal's closet to find something to wear. Royal gets up to follow her. He stands closely behind her while she rummages through the few items of clothing she has in there. She decides on sweats and a t-shirt. She reluctantly turns around to face him.

"Baby— I- I don't know what to say," he admits. "I didn't know she had a baby. I just didn't know-"

"You mean, 'y'all'. Y'all have a baby now," Cleo corrects his words. She maneuvers around him while clutching her outfit. He spins to look at her.

"Promise me you won't leave me. Promise me we'll work through this." Cleo starts getting dressed with her back facing Royal. She leaves him lingering in suspense until her shirt goes over her head.

"You shouldn't concern yourself with that at the moment. You have a child now Royal, something you've always wanted." She walks towards the exit, "Call Lisa, set up visiting time, decorate his room, spend some time with him. You said earlier that you didn't want to be bored. Now, you have a mountain of things to do."

***

Every time a crying spell starts, Cleo practices the breathing techniques she picked up from the emergency room doctor. She's trying her darndest to stay calm, even though she's an emotional wreck right now. She can't let this situation with Royal break her. *She's stronger than that.*

She reaches for her phone and scrolls down her call log. She presses the phone symbol once she makes it to Pedra's name. It rings a few times before she answers.

"Hello?"

"Hey, girl," Cleo says, trying her best to sound like nothing is wrong.

"Hey, girl. What's up?"

"Hey, I was wondering where you go for your prenatal care? I really need a good OB/GYN and I'm having the hardest time locating one."

"Why didn't you call me sooner? Girl, I love my doctor! She's sweet, thorough, knowledgeable, and black. You can't go wrong with her."

"Really? Is she usually booked up? I need to be seen ASAP."

"Nope, and she takes walk-ins. As a matter of fact, I have an appointment with her tomorrow. You can come with me if you want. We can have a pregnant women's day out." Pedra giggles, prompting Cleo to force one out as well.

"Cool. That sounds good. Text me her name and address when you get a chance."

"Absolutely. I'll do it as soon as we hang up."

The ladies talk a few more minutes about nothing in particular. They end their call without Cleo bringing up her newest dilemma with Royal. She doesn't think she'll be able to talk about the DNA test results without disappearing in a puddle of tears. She has to deal with that situation in her own time. She needs to forget about Royal and his other child for the time-being, anyway. *She has her own child to worry about now.*

CHAPTER THIRTY-NINE

Pedra is right, her OB/GYN is the bomb. She caters to Cleo's needs and concerns as if she's the only patient she has. Cleo fills her in on her high-risk situation and the specialist assures her that it's a more common condition than she thinks. As long as she takes it easy, everything will be fine.

Much easier said than done.

Cleo didn't arrive at Dr. Hanks' office in the best mood, but she's leaving with a newfound sense of relief. She has a doctor that she really likes, a prescription for a special type of prenatal vitamin that's supposed to make her morning sickness more tolerable, and an appointment to get an ultrasound in a couple of weeks to get her first peek at her child; *Her and Royal's child.*

Speaking of Royal, he's going to throw a fit once he finds out that Cleo went to her first doctor's appointment without him. She wanted him to be there, but she and him need their space. Honestly, she's still not sure if she can be in the same room with him yet. Him being the father of Lisa's son is a detrimental blow to their brand-new relationship.

She and Pedra are laughing at one of Pedra's jokes when they head towards the parking lot. All of that changes, however, when Royal's name pops up on Cleo's phone screen.

"I have to take this," Cleo informs Pedra in an unenthused way. Pedra looks surprised by Cleo's apparent disgust with her man.

"OK. Well, meet me at the Japanese Bistro. It's right up the street."

The ladies go their separate ways towards their respective vehicles and Cleo answers the phone. She manages to get inside of her truck before Royal responds.

"I'm so sorry you haven't heard from me since yesterday. I broke my cell and I couldn't get a new one until the phone store opened up this morning."

"It's fine," Cleo assures him dryly. She pulls out of the parking lot to follow Pedra's car towards the restaurant.

"Listen, baby— I know things are complicated right now, but I'm sure we'll be able to get through this-"

"Royal, please don't go there. I already told you that I can't deal with that right now. Do you want us to lose our baby?"

"No! Of course I don't! I'm sorry," he exclaims quickly. The silence that follows makes them both uncomfortable.

"So, how is work going? Is your new position being kind to you?" She makes a right turn before answering.

"Actually, I didn't go to work today."

"You didn't? What's wrong? Is everything alright? Shit! I stressed you out yesterday, didn't I?"

"Royal, calm down, it's nothing like that. Actually, I visited an OB/GYN today." Royal gets quiet, making it evident that her words rubbed him the wrong way.

"You had a doctor's appointment today and didn't tell me about it?"

"No— not an appointment, I walked in and they saw me."

"So, you made the decision to go without me, then?"

"I needed to be seen, Royal, especially after last night. I would've called you to let you know, but you broke your phone— remember?"

Royal huffs at her bullshit response. Cleo knows how much he wanted to be at her first doctor's appointment. She went without him to hurt his feelings. *He's not stupid.*

"I understand. I hurt you so now you're trying to hurt me-"

"That's not what this is, Royal, and you know it."

He ignores her.

"So, is the baby doing OK?"

"Yes, the baby is fine."

"Good. Well, I have to go. I was just calling to check on you. If something else comes up regarding our child, please remember to let me know."

"O-" Cleo starts, but the sound of Royal hanging up in her face halts her talking. She removes the phone from her ear with a smack of her lips, "Goodbye to you, too."

The ladies park next to one another in the restaurant's parking lot. Cleo tries to gather herself before exiting her vehicle. She smiles at Pedra, but Pedra isn't buying it. Pedra places her hand on her hip, "I know something is wrong, and it's been that way since last night. If you don't want to talk about it, I can respect that, but you don't have to act like you're OK for me. I want you to be OK for yourself."

Cleo nods her head at her friend before her defenses finally crumble. Tears of frustration appear out of nowhere. Pedra hurries to open her passenger door.

"Get in," she requests. Cleo slides in Pedra's car while Pedra heads to the driver's side. She hands Cleo a napkin as soon as she enters.

"It's OK, Cleo," she says, trying to soothe her friend. Cleo breathes through her emotional breakdown. Pedra rubs her back as a gentle reminder to remain calm. Cleo cries controlled tears until she's able to speak.

"Our baby isn't his first baby, Pedra. He has a fucking two-year-old!" Pedra looks shocked, even though she knew it was a possibility.

"Damn. I'm so sorry to hear that. Wow… that's heavy."

"Very," Cleo agrees with a sniff. Pedra lets out a deep breath.

"So, what are you going to do?"

"I mean, what can I do? The child is his, Pedra. He's obligated to take care of him-"

"No, I mean what are you going to do about Royal? Are you going to stay with him or leave him?" Cleo looks thrown off by the question.

"Pedra, it's not that simple. Am I upset and heartbroken? Very much so, but I'm pregnant by him— and I have his ring on my finger-"

"But Cleo, it is that simple. Look, you can be as upset as you want to be, but if you're not going to leave him, then you have to work on forgiving him. You no longer have the luxury of holding grudges and shit, especially in your condition. Forgive him and move on for your baby's sake."

CHAPTER FORTY

"I think it's interesting that you can't stand the smell of eggs cooking in the morning, but the smell of sushi doesn't bother you."

Cleo smirks at a nauseated Pedra. She demanded a new table after the hostess set them near the sushi bar and Pedra nearly vomited. Cleo found it hilarious.

"You're right. That is interesting, especially since I can't stand the thought of eating sushi. Actually, it smelled amazing. I think I'm going to try some."

"Yeah right. You won't like it, plus you're not supposed to eat raw fish when you're pregnant."

"It doesn't have to be raw. They have a whole side of the menu devoted to cooked sushi… see?" Cleo points to it on Pedra's menu. She rolls her eyes.

"Whatever. Try it. I bet you won't like it."

***

Cleo swallows down her second specialty roll with an amazed Pedra gawking at her. Cleo drops her chopsticks on her empty plate.

"Mm! That was so damn good! I can't believe I've gone this long without trying it," Cleo admits. Pedra shakes her head at her.

"Pregnancy taste buds are completely different from normal ones, at least that's what I've heard anyway."

"Pedra, I've been looking all over for you!" The ladies hear from behind them. They turn around suddenly at the sound of the angry voice.

"Connor!" Pedra shrieks. The ladies watch him and Donte moving in their direction. Cleo's eyes meet Donte's without warning. She immediately breaks their eye contact.

"What the fuck is going on! I've been calling you for days!" Pedra looks around at the nosy faces giving them their undivided attention.

"How did you find me?" She asks in a low tone. Connor stands over her as if he could snatch her up from her seat this very second.

"Don't fucking worry about all of that! The better question is, where the fuck have you been?" She jumps up once Connor's voice reaches a volume not suitable for indoors.

"Maybe we should talk about this outside."

"Maybe you're right," He spits out through clenched teeth. They head towards the restaurant's exit, leaving Donte and Cleo at the table. They look at each other awkwardly.

"Hello, Cleopatra," Donte states while sitting down in Pedra's seat.

"Hello, Donte," she says back. They try their best not to engage with one another, "So, how is life treating you?"

"Life is OK. It could be better," he replies. "What about you? How is that boyfriend of yours treating you?" Cleo nearly chokes at the mention of Royal.

"Well… he's not my boyfriend anymore," she forces out reluctantly. Donte perks up until he spots the diamond ring on her finger. He looks slightly taken aback.

"Wow. I see. Well, congratulations."

"Thank you."

They get quiet when the awkwardness gets thicker than it was before. She looks at him curiously, "How's the dating thing going for you? Have you found someone yet?" Donte stares at her with a serious, but seductive glare. Her heart subtly reacts to the gesture.

"I thought I did, but I guess I was wrong."

"Oh my God! He hit her!" Someone shouts from the front of the restaurant. Donte and Cleo both rush to their feet. They hurry towards the exit to find Pedra sprawled out on the ground. Connor takes a fearful step away from her with tears in his eyes.

"Connor, what the fuck did you do?!" Donte shouts at his brother. Cleo rushes to the side of a hysterical Pedra. She cries loudly in her friend's arms. Cleo glares at Connor furiously.

"I'm calling the fucking police!"

***

"Damn. Then what happened?"

"Connor waited around for the police to show up. When they got there, they handcuffed him and took him to jail. Then, I followed Pedra home to make sure she was OK. She claimed she wasn't hurt, so I left. Now, I'm over here."

Royal looks in the fridge to grab the orange juice. He refills the empty glass sitting in front of Cleo.

"And I'm glad you are."

She sighs before deciding to go there, "Royal, I'm so heartbroken right now, and I don't know what to do about it."

He joins her on the other side of the island and sits down next to her. He turns her body towards his, allowing her legs to rest between his legs. Their positions give off a slight hint of Deja vu. Royal places his hands on her thighs.

"Well, what do you want to do?" She hesitates when she can't immediately produce a response. He takes a deep breath, "Do you want to leave me?"

Her eyes react negatively to the question, "Of course I don't want to leave you."

"Well, are you going to stay with me, then?" Cleo gives him a vulnerable look. He gives her one as well.

"Royal… I'm scared."

"I am, too, especially about this 'being a dad' thing. I went from no kids a month ago to a toddler that I don't even know and a baby on the way. I'm scared shitless."

Cleo starts to feels bad for Royal. All of this time, she's been so caught up in the way she feels that she never tried to look at it from his point of view. She rubs the side of his face as he continues, "I don't know many things, especially about being a father, but I do know that I need you. You do know that, right?"

Cleo nods her head that she does. He grins while wiping the single tear running down her cheek, "Please stand by my side while I get through this. I know that's a lot to ask, but you're my queen. Relationships can't be all flowers and rainbows. There will be trying times, too, and this is one of them."

"I'm here," she whispers, causing him to let out a huge sigh of relief. He leans in and gives her a sensual kiss. Their lips wrap around each other's perfectly. He stands with her hand tucked warmly in his. He leads her towards the stairs.

"Be patient with me, baby. I promise, I'll be worth every second." She stops him before he climbs the first step. He turns around to look at her.

"Are you still going to help me pack?"

"Of course I am, but I thought you wanted to take your time?" She gestures that she changed her mind.

"I think I've taken all of the time I need. I'm ready to move in with you, Royal. I'm ready to start our happily ever after."

[TO BE CONTINUED]

www.ingramcontent.com/pod-product-compliance
Lightning Source LLC
Chambersburg PA
CBHW072134300726
48975CB00003B/1056